Dragon Unleashed

Dragon Point #3

Dragon Point

D1157413

Eve Langlais

New York Times Bestseller

Copyright © September 2016, Eve Langlais
Cover Art by Yocla Designs © August 2016
Edited by Devin Govaere
2nd Edit by Amanda Pederick
Copy Edited by Literally Addicted to Detail
Line Edits by Brieanna Roberston
Produced in Canada

Published by Eve Langlais
1606 Main Street, PO Box 151
Stittsville, Ontario, Canada, K2S1A3
http://www.EveLanglais.com

ISBN: 978 1988 328 51 5

Chapter One

In a hot desert town outside Egypt

Nefarious things were always done at night. Tomas had seen it countless times, and this time would be no different.

As a man who lived in shadows, he expected it. After all, didn't Tomas also move by darkness to accomplish his dirty deeds? And, he should note, those deeds did not come cheap.

Under the cloak of night, Tomas had acquired a tail—not the kind that wagged behind him, he might add. His tail was of the human variety, and he caught them following, but only by chance. Whoever they were, he would commend them before he killed them because they were truly gifted at the art of blending in.

No amateurs these. Their garb was a perfect foil, the fabric worn and dusty. The head covering revealed only the eyes. He might have thought them townspeople if not for the intelligence and rapier tracking of their gazes. The lethargic Bedouins in this small, sleepy town weren't that determined.

The inhabitants of this place also never followed Tomas, not once they knew why he'd come—and it wasn't for the spicy *maqluba* that Hala made fresh every day.

There were other things in this sleepy town that caught his eye. Old things.

I am the man who speaks with ghosts. Not literally. Although, he would add that he found the dead much easier to handle than real people. Real people talked and expected replies. Some wanted to be his friend. As if he'd stoop so low. Bad enough that he had to work among the unknowing masses. Even his team of archeologists—many of them fresh-out-of-school ideologists—grated on his nerves. He would have preferred to study this new scientific site on his own. *I want to keep the secrets for myself.* But in this day and age, appearances had to be kept, and permission given.

I am a modern-day Indian Jones—without the hat, the whip, and the girl. Why waste his time on trappings when Tomas was more interested in other things? Like the past. More specifically, the mysteries lost through time.

Knowledge is priceless.

Tomas wasn't the only one who liked ancient artifacts. Robbers, especially those dealing with rich collectors, wanted to get their grubby hands on his treasures. They could try. It would be the last thing they did.

Tomas couldn't abide robbers. And no, he didn't think of himself as a thief, but rather a collector. As such, he didn't have to abide by the same rules as others. *I am above petty laws,* but since killing people tended to cause problems, he tried to ensure people deserved it—and usually, guaranteed there was no body to find.

In the case of his tail, he magnanimously

decided to see if they deserved a quiet death.

Screaming ones are better for morale. Yes, they were also more fun, but it tended to freak out civilians, and many citizens were armed nowadays.

In the off chance Tomas's paranoia tried to get the better of him—who knew what that last batch of hashish he smoked was laced with—he darted into a stall, fabric stretched on poles framing the entrance to a shop.

The curtain barely rustled when he ducked inside and startled the man eating his dinner. The mustache on the man's upper lip was lush, his skin pockmarked from acne. When the shopkeeper went to stand, Tomas held up a hand.

"Don't stop eating on my account. Finish your meal while I browse your wares." Tomas had not planned to buy anything, but since he needed a reason to linger, he might as well see what was being offered.

The largish room was filled with carpets, most of them rolled tightly, but there were a few lavishly woven pieces hanging on the walls, and another spread out on the floor.

A bright blue mosaic fabric at the top of a pile drew his eyes. Even rolled, the bold patterns appealed. He forgot for a moment why he'd initially come in here—tail, what tail?—and Tomas did what any shopper would. He ordered a carpet—one that he did not need.

I want it.

He would enjoy the new rug in his tent, the thickly woven tapestry a rush of bold color that would brighten his living quarters when they delivered it the next day.

No one else entered the store while he conducted his business. Tomas paid the shopkeeper and then ventured out.

Emerging from the dim interior, he let his eyes adjust to the gloom of the thick night. The glow from a few lanterns was the only thing holding back the deepest darkness. He immediately noticed he'd not lost those following him. It didn't prove difficult to spot furtive movement ahead on the dusty path between dwellings, and the prickling on his nape let him know that another hid somewhere behind and nearby.

Sandwiched. How sporting.

Tomas pretended as if he didn't spot them—wouldn't want to scare them off. He sauntered with feigned casualness to hide the adrenaline that had begun to course through his veins. Finally, a little more excitement than the careful digging, dusting, and sifting of broken bits found in the dirt.

I was so sure I'd find something here. All the signs indicated to the treasure trove being around here somewhere. But he'd yet to find definitive proof.

Frustration wasn't something he handled well, so this group's attempt to shadow him provided a much-needed break in the monotony of his current excavation project.

Foolish thieves. They should have chosen an easier mark. He'd teach them a lesson they wouldn't forget.

With his hands shoved into his pockets, Tomas walked along the dusty path that wound through the eclectic mix of buildings, most built of stone, some of corrugated siding, even a few canvas

tents. He exited the town without being accosted—
a shame—and began heading toward his camp. He
doubted they'd let him get that far.

*Look at me, walking as if I haven't a care in the
world. La-de-fucking-da.* He thought about whistling,
but worried it would be a little too much
insouciance.

The thieves waited for him to reach a curve
in the path, the one that took Tomas out of sight of
town and away from any eyes that might be
watching. A fellow stepped into the middle of the
road and pointed a knife at him. Tomas didn't need
to peer over his shoulder to know his second
pursuer closed the gap. Probably sporting another
blade, or perhaps he was more of a gun-toting chap.
Either way, not good odds…for them.

Lips pulled into a grim smile, Tomas
dropped his knapsack onto the ground. He took a
moment and rolled up his sleeves, the picture of
indifference. In a sense, he was. The challenge
wouldn't last long, and wouldn't even cause him to
break out in a sweat he was sure. Few things
humans did could really make him exert himself.

It was only as the guy with the knife neared
that Tomas realized there was no scent, none at
all—wyverns!—confirming a gleeful fact.

These aren't simple thieves. Because where there
were wyverns, dragons usually followed. What an
excellent evening this was turning out to be. The
most exciting thing to happen since he'd arrived.

His tunic shirt gave him plenty of room to
move in. He dropped into a fighting stance,
limbering up his muscles as he bounced on the balls
of his feet.

"Let's see what you've got." His fist shot out, and the knife guy dodged left, avoiding it. The knife slashed forward, but Tomas blocked it with a blow to the man's wrist. He swung with his other hand and gut punched the fellow. His opponent blew out a hard blast of air and hunched, drawing his shoulders in, his face down.

Crack. Tomas connected his fist to the guy's chin and sent him flying backwards.

He'd no sooner finished the arc of that swing than he ducked and spun, lashing out with his foot and tangling it in the ankles of the second assailant.

In a mere blink, he knelt on the guy's chest, his knees pinning the man's arms, his hands gripping the fellow by the neck. "What do you want? Is it treasure you're after?"

"Now!" yelled the fellow on the ground.

Too late did Tomas realize the trap he'd fallen into. While busy with two weak opponents, the true threat moved in.

The men, dressed in night-blending attire, aimed a series of guns at him. Too many for them all to miss.

But it would be interesting to see how many he could take out before they took him down. He roared as he charged, pulling on his essence, not caring if anyone saw. The seams on his clothes pulled apart then ripped as his true self sought to break free.

The first dart hit, and he kept moving. The second and third still didn't do much. By the fourth and fifth, his body started slowing. By the time he'd gotten hit by his eighth dose of drugs, his eyes were shutting, and his beast let out a wail within his mind—even as it succumbed.

When next Tomas woke, he was in chains, the guest of a madman.

He couldn't have been more delighted. It gave him cart blanche to spill blood and finally indulge in that break he'd been wishing for.

About time I took a vacation.

Chapter Two

I really need a vacation. Or a lobotomy. Anything would be better than what she did right now.

The bright beams of her headlights lit the road where it wound through the forest somewhere in Idaho. A road not on any map. Not on any GPS system. A road that shouldn't exist.

Yet, there it was, with its fresh pavement leading to a building in the woods. A military building no one seemed to know about. An address she couldn't find any information on. A secret closely guarded. But she had her suspicions.

Chandra—short for Chandra Mary Kashmir, born in the United States of an American mother and a Pakistani father—noted the cameras watching her arrival, saw the shadows of men pacing the rooftop, their frames made bulky with body armor, holding rifles to their chests.

What do they guard in the middle of nowhere?

The secretive missive Chandra received had alluded to something big. She was here to find out for sure what it was before blowing the whistle.

She pulled her car to a stop on the wide paved drive. There were no other vehicles outside. Nothing to identify this place. She might not have known it existed if not for the message someone had sent her anonymously.

If you're still looking for answers, then follow this. This being a set of coordinates that, when punched in, showed nothing on any map. Nothing was supposed to be here, which was why she'd decided to go see in person.

From the nondescript building—the exterior a bland, beige siding and lacking windows of any kind—a short and rather rotund fellow wearing a suit, replete with a tie, emerged. He didn't wear a uniform, and yet he kept his hair military short and his shoulders back. The expression on his jowly face seemed quite stern. It didn't bode well that he carried a clipboard as he approached. Having met men with clipboards in the past, she found them to be rather pompous and condescending.

"State your business," he demanded, his words somewhat muffled by the glass.

Time to see if the drama classes she'd taken in high school stuck. She rolled down her window and tilted her lips into a vacuous smile. "Oh, thank goodness. I am so happy to finally find someone. I seem to have lost my way."

"I'll say. You're on restricted property, ma'am."

Ma'am. So military. "Restricted property? Really? How exciting." Did she look excited with her batting lashes, or as if she'd caught a bug in her eye?

"You'll need to turn around and head back."

"But…" She bit her lower lip. "It's so far. And I really"—her gaze dropped—"have to, you know,"—she lowered her voice—"*go.*"

"You're only thirty minutes or so from town."

She squirmed in her seat. "I don't know if I can last that long, and it's so dark and scary outside." That time she put her lashes into super-twitch mode.

To her surprise, it worked. Probably because the man with the clipboard needed glasses.

He sighed. "Fine. You may come in and use the washroom. But quickly. You're not supposed to be here, and that means I'll have to file a report."

"What is *here*, anyhow?" she asked as she exited her car and followed the man into the building—the middle of her back tickled as she imagined more than a few guns training their sights on her. This adventure was more real and frightening than she'd expected when curiosity had brought her out to take a peek. She worked as a scientist. A doctor of biology. Conspiracies and armed men and secret labs were things for the movies. It didn't happen in real life. She reminded herself of that as fear threatened to swamp her.

How easily they could make her disappear. Without a trace. Gulp.

"We're nothing important. Just an observation facility." The man with the clipboard nodded to another fellow armed on the far side of the room, sentinel to a pair of elevator doors.

"Observing what? There's not much to see out here." She uttered a giggle that sounded completely false to her. Did he hear the insincerity?

"We have been charged with exploring the migratory tendencies of nearby herds of deer." He recited it with a straight face, even though he had to know how strange it sounded given the armed guards outside.

Then again, strange seemed to be the norm these days.

And that's why I'm here. To find out what's going on. Once she gleaned something, then she could act.

Since she'd arrived in this small town as part of a lucrative contract to work for the up-and-coming Lytropia Institute, she'd done nothing but see strange things. Things she'd never imagined. Things like evidence of a secret lab experimenting on...something. Or someone. Of that part, she wasn't entirely sure.

Not long after she'd begun working, she received a video, a glimpse really, of a man. At least, she assumed it was a man. The lighting was bad, the video grainy as it tried to see through shadows. The shape was right for a human male, but the eyes... His eyes glowed, the pits of them green with fire.

Those eyes, as much as his plight, called to her. Who was this man who appeared a prisoner? The tiny clip of video and the mystery compelled her to act.

I'm nuts. Investigating the origin of a video, without backup or any kind of experience outside a lab, and all because some eyes captivated her.

Despite the creepy vibe the place instilled, the inside of the building—the one that still made no sense in the middle of nowhere—proved uninteresting. A reception-type desk took pride of place and appeared to be the only visible piece of furniture. It didn't reveal anything. Built of simple pine, no logo covered its surface. Nothing marred the smooth top of the counter either. Behind the desk, she noted a single stool and a door.

That was it. No cages with creatures inside. No mysterious hum or ominous screams. She didn't even get a chill; the temperature was quite pleasant.

"The bathroom is through there." The man with the clipboard pointed to the door.

With nothing to see, there was no point in stalling.

"Thank you." She entered the small two-piece bathroom and wondered what to do next.

She immediately turned on the water and paced the tiny space. One step, turn. One step, turn.

She didn't use the toilet. First, because she doubted she could go; and second, because she didn't want to be caught with her pants down. Literally.

Her sense of unease grew. There was something wrong here. She knew it. This place hid something. Something big. No one went to this much trouble to hide a report on the deer population—unless they were mutant deer with deadly superpowers.

It could happen. Humanity had recently discovered how much they didn't know when the shapeshifters in the world came out and revealed their presence to the general population.

Shapeshifters, as in people who could change his or her body into something else—usually a large animal. It boggled the mind.

As a doctor, the very thought that a body—one made of the same flesh and bone and blood she possessed—could reshape itself so completely, so perfectly, seemed impossible. The kind of science—and magic— that involved fascinated. It also frightened.

Despite reassurances by the shapeshifting community that their genetic condition wasn't a virus, but something they were born with, Chandra had to wonder. Science was always evolving. Discovering. *Imagine what some people could do if they figured out how the shift is done.*

Which led her back to the man with the fiery green eyes. Was he a shapeshifter being kept prisoner for experimental reasons? And why tell Chandra? She worked simply as a research biologist for Lytropia Institute. At least she used to work for them. The place had undergone some drastic changes, and now it seemed no one had a job.

So why not go exploring weird tips without backup?

I am so stupid. She turned off the water and took a few breaths. There was no mirror to reflect her angst back to her.

I think I might have made a mistake coming here.

In her defense, she'd not known what to expect when she followed the coordinates. This kind of stuff didn't happen in reality. This was movie material.

At any moment, she expected Jason Bourne or someone else to come barreling into the place, guns blazing, looking hot.

The door remained closed. Real life sucked like that. And because this was real life, it meant there was a perfectly logical answer for everything. She was overreacting and letting her imagination run wild.

What would really happen next was she'd walk out of this bathroom, thank the man with the clipboard for the use of the washroom, and return to her car.

There would be no further exploring. *I am done and getting out of here.*

As she exited the bathroom, it didn't take a word for her to realize that she'd overstayed her welcome.

The man with the clipboard bore a frown. "You need to hurry and leave now. Time for you to go back to town and forget you saw this place."

He gripped her arm and guided her. Her steps matched his as he led her through the door outside.

She was leaving, exactly what she wanted, and yet she couldn't help but ask, "What are you hiding? Do you need help?" Because she saw a glimpse of something in his eyes, heard it in his voice. Fear. The fact that he'd let it show frightened her. But the thing that truly made her blood run cold was the pity she also noticed in his gaze.

"No idea what you're implying, ma'am. We have nothing to hide here." Said with a bright smile. The reassurance rang false. "If you think our security is a bit tight, it's just because we don't need any eco nuts barging in and screwing things up."

"Environmentalists are why you have guards on the roof?" She blinked. "You can't seriously tell me they're supposed to shoot the people who want to save the earth from people studying deer." That was a bit much to expect anyone to believe.

The genial smile dropped, and his gaze turned hard. "You have to go. Now. And don't stop for anything," he admonished as he held open the door to her car.

Before she got in, she couldn't help but ask, "What's really going on here?"

"You don't want to know."

"It doesn't seem like it's a good place." She lowered her voice. "You should get out while you can."

"It's too late for us. And for you."

For some reason, his bleak words gave her a chill.

She jumped into the driver seat, and the door slammed shut. She might have held the key too long when she started the engine, the whining scream reminding her to let go. She drove a lot faster leaving than coming in. She clutched the wheel tightly, and she realized she hunched, her breaths coming fast yet shallow.

I made it. I got out. For some reason, that realization didn't completely reassure.

For a few stressful minutes, she watched her mirrors, looking for a tail, headlights behind her. The road remained dark.

I really did escape. Time to dial a friend.

Dex, a guy who worked at Lytropia Institute with her, answered. "Yeah."

"I think I messed up. They're on to me," Chandra rushed into saying without even the pretense of polite niceties.

His tone became very serious. "Where are you?"

In trouble? "In the woods. I went looking for that thing I told you about." She kept it vague. While she had escaped, her paranoia still managed to reach record heights. A part of her couldn't help but wonder if someone could be monitoring her calls.

"Idiot! Why would you do that?" Dex exclaimed. "Give me your coordinates. I'll come get you."

And do what? She almost asked but paused as she heard a woman through the connection say, "I'm coming, too."

Dex had someone with him. Probably that crazy woman—Adi something or other with the crazy-colored hair—who'd had a jealous fit when Chandra had a dinner meeting with Dex.

Tangling with the crazy girl with short hair after the night she'd had did not appeal. "Don't bother leaving where you are. I'm in my car. It's best if I meet you. Where are you?"

He named an address that she kind of made note of. She didn't plan on meeting up. She'd probably just text him on her way through town because she was leaving.

I am done playing this game of spy. She wasn't a spy, but a scientist. First thing she'd do when she got home—her *real* home back in San Fran—she'd send that video and those coordinates off to someone she knew who worked in law enforcement. Let them decide if there was a case to investigate. She was going back to studying things through a microscope.

Hanging up with Dex, Chandra tossed her phone on the seat beside her. She tried to reassure herself that everything was fine.

She'd left. What was the worst thing that could happen to her? She'd not technically trespassed. There were no signs. She'd not touched a thing.

What if it has to do with national security? Because those guys with guns were serious protection. They could have been military, and if that were the case, they had certain rules to follow. "I am a law-abiding citizen. They can't arrest me, and even if they do, I've done nothing wrong." They couldn't hurt her—so long as they were legit and following the edicts of the law.

What if they didn't? What if she'd stumbled onto something big, say like an organization that didn't believe in leaving witnesses behind?

What if—

Something swooped suddenly across the hood of her car, a shadow with wings that caused her to scream and slam on the brakes.

What was that?

She sat there, breathing hard, staring out the windshield, the beams of her lights illuminating the road and nothing else. But she'd seen something.

Probably a bird or a bat.

A big freaking bird or bat.

Perhaps she'd seen an owl. They were large and nocturnal.

Thump.

Something hit the top of her vehicle, and she looked up then kept staring as the top of her car bulged, the metal bending under some weight. Her eyes grew so wide, she was surprised they stayed in her head.

What's on top of my car? She gripped the wheel tightly and held her breath as she heard whatever it was that had landed on her vehicle move around.

Just a bird. Nothing to be scared of.

She pressed the accelerator, increasing her

speed, hoping to dislodge whatever it was. She heard a disturbing sound, a crunch and creaking as the roof caved in further.

She braced herself as she slammed on the brakes, the tires screaming, the car sliding. With a wrenching noise of metal, something went flying off her roof and soared past the beams of her headlights.

It's gone. I got it off.

She smiled.

Thump. She couldn't help the startled squeak that came out of her.

"I'm safe in here. It can't get to me." The car would protect her, and tomorrow, she'd laugh at how the big, bad bird had scared her.

Tomorrow. Sure. Right now, she wished she'd peed when she had the chance.

More creaking and popping of metal accompanied the movements of the thing on top of her car. She didn't even want to think of the damage. Would insurance cover an attack by an owl?

That thing that flew off wasn't an owl. And neither, she'd wager, was the friend it had brought along.

It looked more demonic than that.

Did she have a clause against demon attacks? She almost giggled at the inane thought.

She lost all urge to laugh as a thing, and she meant *thing*, swooped in from the side and landed on her hood. The sight of it froze her blood and dropped her jaw.

Dear, Devi—the goddess she prayed to. *Help me*—for she faced evil.

A *raakshas* stood on her hood, a demon. What else could it be with its dark, squat body, wings, and the ugly face made terrifying with all those sharp teeth?

Her hand slapped the door lock button; the sudden click sealing her in, a false security.

The action drew attention, and a smirk formed on the demon's face.

The creature crouched down, its human eyes made more frightening by his monstrous visage. It knocked on the window.

She whispered, "Nobody's here."

The words of a coward. Her *daadee*, her mother's mother, would have known what to do. She would have cuffed Chandra and told her to stop being a ninny. You were only a victim if you didn't try.

"I am not a victim." Chandra had fought too hard to get where she was to let anything, even a demon, get in her way.

She slammed the car from park into drive, and her foot hammered the gas. The vehicle shot forward, fast enough that her hood surfer couldn't keep his feet and he hit her windshield first before rolling up it and over the roof of her car, taking the roof creature with him. The impact left behind a lovely crack, but Chandra didn't care.

She drove as if the demons of hell were after her, and in a sense, they were. Even over the scream of the engine, she could hear a strange, ululating sound. The high, piercing shriek of a predator on the chase.

I am its prey.

She might have squeaked at the thought.

Hands sweaty, Chandra gripped the steering wheel and leaned forward, willing the town to be closer. Surely, among the lights and buildings, monsters thought to belong in fables wouldn't dare follow.

Alas, she wasn't fated to make it that far.

Something came at her, from straight-ahead, a group of flying imps, and she screamed. Screamed as she swerved and braked.

The demons hit her car, and it rocked on two wheels before slamming down. She gripped the wheel and hit the gas pedal, but the car wouldn't move, probably because a pair of the demons had lifted the front end of her vehicle, which meant her wheels spun uselessly.

A demon, his eyes alight with glee—made all the more frightening because they were human eyes—pressed his face against her side window. Humanoid eyes in the face of a monster glared at her with a savage glee. It grabbed at the handle for her door and pulled. The lock kept it shut.

Smash.

While she'd watched the demon on her side, another had punched through the passenger window and clicked the lock.

The one at her window smiled.

She smiled back, and when he pulled open the door, she withdrew her hand from her purse with her can of pepper spray and got it in the face.

It let out an unearthly shriek and reeled away from the door. She didn't stick around to enjoy her small victory. With the safety of the car compromised, she dove out of the vehicle and ran back in the direction of the building where there were men with guns.

No wonder they had guns. There were monsters in these woods!

She ran as best she could, her low-heeled shoes not ideal, and her speed far below Olympic standards. She huffed and puffed and pumped her legs, expecting to be attacked at any moment.

She heard the creatures' strange cries and saw the furtive shift of shadows out of the corner of her eye, but they didn't accost her. They could have, and yet, they seemed more intent on harassing her, their howling cries shrill and mocking as they dipped overhead and ghosted through the tree line edging the road—moving shadows of menace.

Her breath heaved as she ran. The stitch in her side was ignored.

What had taken five minutes to drive took her much longer to run, all the while harassed by the demons.

But alive. So inexplicably alive, and she refused to listen to the little voice that insisted they were herding her.

She could have sobbed with relief when she spotted the building in the distance, the low glow of the single outdoor light a symbol of hope.

Help. Finally.

Except the men on the roof were gone. How could they go? The monsters were here.

She ran to the door and pounded on it. Pounded and banged and cried, but the man with the clipboard didn't open it. No one did.

She rolled around until her back leaned against the building. She eyed the darkness outside the cone of light. How many of the demons approached? Would they attack at once, or toy with her like many a predator did with its prey?

Fear had her body taut with tension, but at the same time, adrenaline coursed through her veins. She wouldn't give in without a fight.

"You really shouldn't have come here."

The words came from her left, and a turning of her head brought into view the rotund fellow, wearing a lot less clothing than earlier and minus his clipboard.

A stranger's naked bits dangling? She could handle it, and politeness should have made her avert her gaze, but she couldn't, not once she noticed his eyes.

Devi, help me. She recognized those eyes. The *raakshas.*

Chapter Three

Clink. Clink. Scuff. Clink. The chain rattled a discordant song every time Tomas moved, a reminder of his status. A prisoner.

How degrading. Didn't they respect who he was? *What* he was...

Of course not, or they would have never dared to capture him in the first place.

It made him thirsty.

For blood.

Actually, he craved a fine bottle of wine, but that didn't mean he'd disregard the blood thing. There was always a need to spill more blood. Fresh and hot was best.

Damn, I'm hungry. Tomas had grown a tad gaunt during his stay. He didn't get much meat here. He didn't get much to eat at all. The spartan existence proved rather refreshing. Relaxing.

With only a cursory curiosity, Tomas wondered what day it was. He could never be entirely sure. The drugs they pumped into his system sometimes put him under for days. He'd not rested so well in years.

Lots of sleep, though, meant he needed to catch up when he woke. He learned not to choke the technicians drawing his blood too long, else they had difficulties answering.

Like it was his fault they were so fragile.

The humans who worked here kept him full of drugs, lots of drugs, because when Tomas wasn't sleeping, he tended to get frisky. And when he got frisky, people sometimes died. Usually screaming, in a puddle of warm blood.

Tasty for him, not so much for them.

Humans were so slow and easily scared. Not really much of an opponent for someone like Tomas. What made them dangerous was they didn't fight fair.

The cowards kept Tomas in a stoned stupor because they knew he could demolish them. In that, they respected his superiority.

Because I am great. It was why the universe revolved around him.

The silly humans might think Tomas chained and a prisoner, but the truth was, Tomas bided his time. He knew his value. Knew they wouldn't kill him. Not yet.

Those in the secret lab they kept him in wanted something from Tomas. However, he'd yet to figure out what. What did they steal from him while he slept? And why?

He should note that, while it was mostly humans working in this hidden lab, the one in charge of it all—the man Tomas would delight in tearing limb from limb and then roasting with some fine herbs for dinner later—was anything but human.

Theodore Parker ran this secret lab. He was the boss. A werewolf shifter by birth, a businessman in pharmaceuticals, Mr. Theodore

Parker had branched out into medical experimentation, assassination, and basic grandeur plans of world domination. He had to be stopped.

The world is mine. Usually, Tomas didn't dine on canine, but in this instance, he'd make an exception. Grandfather would be so proud. He'd raised Tomas old school, and that meant eating the enemy to take on his strength. Thankfully, Grandmother knew how to make them tasty.

After the ignobleness of being caught by a shifter—*I will enjoy eating your eyeballs, Theo Parker*—Tomas needed some grand gesture to restore his reputation.

What a shame that Parker never got close enough for Tomas to take a bite, even though Tomas had asked nicely. "Here, boy. Where's my good dog? Won't you come down, little puppy, and see how big my eyes are?" Tomas teased in his gruffest voice. He used the acoustics in the room to his advantage and was rewarded with the sharp intakes of breath by the humans watching.

Let them stew a while in their fear. It would tenderize them for later.

Parker didn't come down to visit, which really put a crimp in Tomas's mouth-watering urge for a wolf rump roast. *When I'm done, I'll floss my teeth with his bones.*

Alas, sly and wily Parker knew better than to get within reach, but the man—who would become the new rug for Tomas's mudroom—did enjoy watching.

At least, he used to. It had been a while since Tomas had seen Parker. The man kept busy; evil was more work than people realized.

Standing, the chains tethering Tomas rattled again, but he ignored their weight and noise in order to stretch. There wasn't much else for him to do in the pit, which sounded as stark as the reality. A deep hole, the walls sheer, and close enough that he couldn't take his true shape and fly. No mattress to pillow his body. Not even a blanket to warm his frame.

Escape seemed impossible with no ladder leading up. The glassy surface of the walls proved too slippery to grip. Assuming he could break free from the chains.

I could. But no use letting his supposed captors know that their attempt to hold him had a flaw. *A big flaw.* Their puny measures wouldn't hold him when the time came.

The time is coming soon.

Since his capture, Tomas hadn't learned anything. He was, however, well rested and bored. So very bored.

Let's go kill something.

His inner spirit knew exactly what it wanted to do.

Stretching his arms, he paced the small area, refusing to glance upward, even though he felt the weighty stare of people watching.

Let them watch.

Let them tremble.

Let them wonder if today is the day Tomas will send them to their maker.

"Don't tell me you still have hope, Tomas?" Parker's mocking words echoed down from speakers placed at the upper rim of the pit. "You can't escape."

"Is that a challenge?" He liked to collect those. Personal achievements were some of his most treasured possessions.

"When will you admit you've lost?"

"How do you figure I've lost?" Tomas raised his head, the scalp of it shorn. It didn't please him that his head felt bereft without the lush mantle of hair he'd once sported. The scientists here kept him clean-shaven, mostly to prevent the infestation of lice and other critters. How kind of them.

Just another reason to kill them.

And drink from their skulls. Barbaric, but hey, he wasn't about to argue with his other side. It was, after all, a time-honored tradition with defeated enemies.

"You show such optimism," Theo remarked, the various embedded speakers making his words echo. "And yet, it's been what now, three months? You've tried a few times to escape. Killed some good people and never managed to make it out. Admit it." Theo's voice lowered an octave. "I have beaten you. I am in control."

"Don't get too ahead of your masters there, puppy." A deliberate goad that gave Tomas great pleasure. "I am simply enjoying your hospitality. I have not slept this much in years. I feel wonderful. Refreshed. I should thank you and offer to pay for this wondrous experience." Tomas leaned against the wall.

"So your screams during our last round of experiments were of pleasure, then?"

At the reminder of the excruciating pain, Tomas bared his teeth, and his beast, that inner raging monster, briefly rose to the surface. But that was as far as he allowed it. He knew what Parker was after, and he wouldn't give in.

What had happened was something he'd rather not recall. But Tomas also wasn't so weak that he'd whine about it. He played the victim to find out what happened. Firsthand was one of the best ways to figure things out.

"You wouldn't have to suffer if you'd just shift."

Parker's end goal. He wanted Tomas to change into his true shape. Like hell. *No one makes me do anything.*

"Kind of hard for me to transform when you've always got me sleeping." Although Parker had almost managed to force Tomas to morph during his last comatose round. Thankfully, Tomas had woken in time to stop it.

"The way I hear it, you woke early and maimed our newest attending scientist."

"Maimed? I must have missed. I was aiming to kill. My mistake. It won't happen again."

"Why are you so stubborn?" The restrained tone cracked slightly. "I can stop the pain and give you so much if you would just shift."

Just. It sounded so simple. Parker wanted blood samples in a shifted state, his true state. Dangerous stuff his blood, which was why Parker wasn't getting it.

However, Tomas didn't let him know that. "So if I do as you ask, you'll stop the torture sessions?" Which he healed from with only a few new scars. "Feed me decent carnivore meals rather than this protein bar crap?"

"I can do that."

"What about a woman? As you noted, it's been a while."

"I can get a woman for you and all the rest. Shift." Parker hastened to add. "And promise you'll let us close enough to get some samples."

"You can have the samples you want if you come down here. Right here." Tomas jerked his thumb to a spot in front of him.

"I'm not a pet that you can order around." The words hissed out. "And you are useless to me in this form."

"Then let me go."

"Never. You will change eventually. My scientists have been perfecting the formula. Soon, you won't be able to say no, and I will have what I need."

"What you need is your head shoved up your ass because, apparently, you refuse to see how full of shit you are."

"Have it your way, Tomas. The painful way." Parker turned off the speaker, but Tomas didn't have to hear him to know what he said next. *Drug him.*

There was no escaping the mist with the medicinal scent. No hiding from its effects.

Now, as other times, he couldn't hold his breath forever, and he slumped to the floor.

It seemed like but a blink of his eyes, and yet it must have been much longer, for he woke strapped to a gurney. His lids felt heavy, and so he squinted, but he didn't see much, not with his lashes so thick he could barely see through them.

Those lashes, though, served to hide. He peeked through the tiny, obscured slit and recognized the heavily shielded room: no windows, one door—metal, bolted shut and requiring a keycard for access. A few cameras monitored the room, and the guards watching only needed to press one button to send Tomas back to Sleepy Land.

Movement and a rustle of fabric drew his attention to a spot behind his head, but he still didn't move, pretending the drugs were still running too thickly through his system.

No point in letting anyone know Tomas once more processed their attempts to sedate, and even more quickly than before. They'd already changed his dosage and the mixture numerous times trying to counter his ability to filter it, but his body was stronger than any drug.

There's a reason I'm better than you, Parker. I know how to play the long game.

He continued to feign unconsciousness, letting himself peek only through the slimmest of slits. He took stock of his body, noting the IVs digging into each of his arms. The clear one, a hydrating solution to keep him alive. The other pumped some noxious cocktail into his veins. Parker was determined to make him shift. *So he can steal my DNA.*

Not happening. Tomas knew the merits of paranoia and protecting his secret. Grandfather had drilled him growing up and stressed the importance of hiding from the humans.

Tomas learned early in his adulthood that the humans knew more than his grandfather realized. But those who knew didn't out the shifters of the world. Didn't expose those who lived under a strange veil of normalcy.

Everyone had lived in ignorant bliss until the day Parker decided to thrust the existence of cryptozoids upon the world. Shifters first, then the fairies and merpeople. Tomas even heard rumblings that dragons were coming out.

The craziness. Was nothing sacred anymore?

More noise as material crinkled. White fabric moved into view, and Tomas flexed his fingers, wondering if the person would move close enough for him to have some fun.

A scent caught him, deeply exotic, making him think of the heated desert sands and spice. Cinnamon and nutmeg. Delicious.

I want it. Craved it. He couldn't help but sniff again.

The uncontrollable interest took him by surprise. *I need to slow down.*

No. Smells yummy, he argued with himself.

He wanted a bite. Roasted was normally his choice. Nothing better than crispy skin to crunch. But in this case, he'd settle for nibbling the spice-scented skin.

The figure moved away, and he heard mumbling. "Wrong. So wrong."

What was wrong? And why did her voice tickle over him, drawing a frisson from his skin? Yes, her. The soft, feminine voice with only the slightest hint of an accent gave it away.

"How did I ever think this would work?"

Her castigation almost made him smirk. Hard to feel pity that the doctor's formula did not work as expected.

A hand touched him, and he almost flinched

at the electric contact. How long since someone had touched him? Surely that explained why his senses were roused by such a simple act.

"You poor thing. What is wrong with Parker? Why would he do this to you?"

Pity? That almost had him casting off his feigned act of sleep.

"Do you even know what they're trying to do?"

No, but keep talking. He'd love to find out.

She sighed. "I certainly don't know. Parker won't tell me anything. And the few others I've met are just as clueless."

Yeah, that irritates me, too. What was the point of terrifying people into talking when they couldn't relate anything of worth?

"Why do they have you tied down? Drugged. What makes you so dangerous?" Again, a finger trailed over his skin, running along the edge of his hair, ending at his jaw.

Did she even grasp how dangerous her act was? Had no one explained he could kill her with one hand and not feel bad about it?

Then why haven't I killed her yet?

He could. Even tied to a bed, he was deadly, and yet Tomas didn't act. He didn't move. He didn't do a damned thing but let her stroke him. And talk—her melodious voice the nicest thing he'd heard since his capture.

Nicer would be her hand moving farther down.

"I was such an idiot. Thinking I could come here and expose what was happening. Stupid. I know. And now I'm just as much a prisoner as you."

Hardly. She wore the white coat, and yet for some reason, her sad words made him want to rise and smite those that made her feel that way.

Grind their bones to dust.

Her fingers brushed imaginary hair from his forehead. "I should stop wasting time and draw your blood. Parker gets very upset when I dally too long. He seems to think you're becoming immune to the drugs. Doubtful. He's pumped you full of enough stuff to take down an elephant."

An elephant? The comparison almost brought forth a growl.

Perhaps she's admired my massive trunk. That brought a twitch to a part of his body that had played dead since his arrival.

Not dead, obviously, but still, lusting after the enemy? The drugs must be working some kind of evil magic. Perhaps they'd infected him with an erectile remedy that would keep him in a constant state of arousal that required him to leap from this bed and take the woman they'd so kindly offered.

I can't just pounce on her.

Women tended to scream when a male did that. That tidbit had arrived via his great-uncle Vinny. He'd had more women divorce him than Tomas had dated.

Something pricked his arm, and he could smell—over the astringent antiseptic—the coppery scent of blood. His blood.

Always with his blood. Vials and vials of it taken, and for no reason. *Don't they know my blood is useless in this form?* Apparently not, because they kept trying, which was really stupid of them. *They really shouldn't provoke me.* He would have his revenge.

He must have moved, perhaps uttered a sound, because he practically felt it when she froze. The very air seemed to grow taut with anticipation—and fear.

Her fear. "Are you awake?" She whispered the words, and yet he knew those watching would hear.

No use feigning sleep. He opened his eyes and smiled, showing all his teeth. "Hello, doctor."

She gaped at him, blinked thickly lashed lids over giant brown eyes. She didn't scream or run. Her lips, full and a red that came from nibbling, quirked. "Hello."

One tiny word. It slapped him. He might have recoiled. He certainly felt off balance, and Tomas didn't like it one bit.

"You're new," he stated.

"I am. But I hear you're not."

Did the doctor think to play nice with the prisoner? He wasn't that foolish. "Don't play games with me, doctor. It won't work."

"Neither will your bully tactics." She moved away from him.

He didn't like her moving away. *Then let's go get her.* The bed and the straps holding him thought to keep him away.

Nothing can keep me from her. Tomas pulled on his beast side with no hesitation, took the strength he needed, and then pushed upwards. His hands formed fists, the cords in his arms and wrists straining. Metal groaned, and he startled a gasp from the caramel-skinned doctor.

Snap. Snap. His arms came loose, which meant it took only a little extra time to free his legs.

I'm not contained, you fuckers. Tomas stood and wondered when the gas would begin to seep.

He immediately frowned. They couldn't do the gas. It might hurt the woman. Oddly enough, he found himself averse to the idea.

Currently, the doctor with the exotic accent stared at him, so it seemed only right to stare right back. It allowed him time to catalogue—and process—her fragile beauty. She was average height, which meant up to his chin, with a slim frame covered in tanned skin.

Skin I need to taste.

Except, he didn't just think she'd taste delicious basted with avocado oil and spices and roasted over a slow, coal-burning fire. *I bet her skin is lovely to lick. And what of the honey pot between her legs?*

Lick some honey or lose himself to chocolate as he stared into the lustrous depths of her brown eyes? He couldn't decide. Full red lips parted, drawing his gaze. Wanted them. On him.

"Are you going to kill me?" She spoke and caught him off guard.

"I should kill you. I don't like doctors."

"I'm a biologist."

"Same thing. It's not nice to experiment on people."

"I didn't experiment."

"Yet you are in the room with me and saw the stuff being pumped into me. You cannot tell me that the stuff in that bag is anything my body needs." He waved to the IV.

"I don't know what it is. I was just asked to draw some samples."

"Do you always take samples from

unconscious people?"

"Parker says you're not a person."

"What does Parker say I am?" He smiled and again bared his pearly whites to no reaction.

She held his gaze, seemingly steady, yet he could scent the undercurrent of fear, see the fast, thready beat of her pulse. "He hasn't said what you are, just that you're dangerous."

"I am."

Her head tilted. "Perhaps even more dangerous than he realizes."

"I think you're right." His lips twitched, rueful and teasing. "What a shame a smart woman like you works for a man like him."

Before she could reply, and he could tell she wanted to, a familiar male voice erupted from the embedded speakers. "Dr. Kashmir works for me because she knows what's good for her. Don't you, doctor?"

It seemed Parker was watching today. How interesting.

The woman raised her gaze to the ceiling and glared. "I hope you die from some kind of incurable itch."

Not a solution that involved spurting copious amounts of blood, but Tomas admired the insulting elegance and pure torture of it.

Tomas felt a need to show the doctor he could be quite vindictive, too. "I've offered to eviscerate him, but that twat waffle with a yellow belly turned me down."

She shook her head. "He was right to turn you down. And you should know better. Evisceration is rather messy and won't prevent him from returning as a zombie."

He almost laughed. "You believe in zombies?"

"Doesn't everyone?"

A scientist believed? His brows lifted. "You know of someone who has managed to recreate the resurrection formula?"

Her grin proved endearingly cheeky. "Nope. But I am fascinated that you thought I might have. And what do you mean *recreate*?"

Parker interrupted. "While you're chatting, why not make yourselves useful. Doctor Kashmir, please retrieve the samples we requested. And if the patient cooperates, perform a full physical."

Cooperate? The usual answer was no, but in this case... "I'll go along with it, but only if she forgoes the gloves." He turned and positioned himself on the gurney. He peeled off the pale blue, linen smock top he wore, revealing his upper body.

Her mouth rounded, not in awe but displeasure. "Why are you so gaunt? A man your size should have a thicker frame."

"I still have my muscle." He flexed for her, showing the firm cord without an ounce of fat. Looking down at himself, he noted how tight his skin was to his body, delineating every tendon and bone.

He needed more food.

"Someone give this man a steak." She echoed his sentiment.

"Nothing wrong with this body, doctor. Touch me and see." He dared.

Her hands tucked behind her back instead. It appeared as if she was not prepared for him and didn't know how to handle him.

But I know how to handle you. Licking a sticky sweet sauce off her body came to mind.

"You'll have to move away from the door if you're going to examine me, doctor," he chided.

She remained pressed against the locked portal. "You're being too amenable. What are you planning?"

"What can I plan? I'm a prisoner and patient at your complete mercy." He did not think he managed unassuming. Given the biting of her lower lip, she appeared rather unconvinced of his benign nature.

"You broke out of your straps."

"Don't blame me for that. You would hate them, too, if you were a prisoner."

"I am a prisoner."

The lie angered him more than it should have. "You're wearing the white coat. You can walk out that door at any time." Technically, so could he. It was the bullets on the other side that concerned him a little. "You have a life, whereas I have the pit."

"That's you in there?" She appeared genuinely shocked. "Are you alone? Do you have a, um, pitmate?"

"Does it look like I have a roommate? I'm alone. This whole lab is centered around me. Or haven't you noticed the lack of others to play with?"

"I haven't been out much. Just here and my quarters. And once, the control room."

Probably another lie made to make her seem stuck. Tomas began to grasp Parker's devious plot.

It wouldn't work.

"I'm getting cold over here, doctor." He spread his arms. "Are we going to do this or not? Although, I warn you, the chill might make it so a certain measurement of length is inaccurate. I'm sure we could fix that, though, if you gave me a hand." Crude, and not his usual style, but an urge to grab at the doctor meant a higher level of frustration than expected when she refused to come near him.

She didn't move from her spot against the door. "Why does Parker keep you here?"

"You tell me."

"I don't even know who you are."

"More lies?" He *tsked* her. He doubted Parker would have brought her here and left her blind as to what Tomas was.

"I'm not lying. I have no idea who you are. You're not who I expected to find, actually."

She'd expected another? A hot flash of jealousy almost made him lose control. Tomas tempered it. "Sorry you feel so deprived. Is this where I tell you that I'm better than anyone else? To choose me?" He snorted. "You are attractive and quite tasty, I'm sure, but I haven't lost my wits." Her feminine wiles wouldn't break him.

"You might want a second opinion on that," she muttered, her slight accent adding a delightful twist to the insult.

She played her role of innocent so well. It angered him. "Is this my carrot, Parker?" he asked aloud, hiding any traces of frustration. "I know I asked you for a woman, but I expected someone less dressed. At least she's pretty, not that I'll see her face when I take her from behind." He tossed the threat to the ceiling and the camera furiously recording from up there. As he did, he missed her approach—and the slap.

Crack.

Chapter Four

Uh-oh. Chandra realized her mistake a moment after her hand connected with the rock-hard jaw.

Sure, the patient had insulted her. Yes, he deserved it. But she might have forgotten she was in a room with a killer—or so the guards had claimed when they'd escorted her here.

"Whatever you do, don't get within arm's reach. He bites." The guard pointed to a missing earlobe, and she'd almost bitten her own tongue when her teeth clacked shut in shock.

She'd forgotten the warning. Not only had she gotten too close, but she'd also slapped him.

As a person whose father—sometimes with a heavy hand—had taught her to own her actions and stand her ground, she lifted her chin. "You will apologize."

His eyes narrowed. "Shouldn't I be asking that of you?"

"I've done nothing, but you insinuating that I am a whore is unacceptable. I am not here to give you sexual pleasure, or for you to threaten me. It's rude, and I won't stand for it."

"You won't stand for it." He repeated her words with incredulity. His hand shot out, and his fingers—his long and strong fingers—gripped the column of her throat. "Do you realize how easily I could crush it?"

"Seems rather extreme, especially given you're wrong." It took every ounce of bravery she possessed to reply. But she knew better than to back down before a predator. Sometimes bravery—and extreme stupidity—was the only thing they responded to.

"Are you suicidal?" His fingers tensed.

"I should hope not since I finally paid off my student loans and I'd like to enjoy that extra money each month."

He released her, and she had to fight to stand her ground rather than dart across the room for distance.

"Why are you here?" He turned the tables and questioned her.

"Because I went poking my nose where I shouldn't have." It didn't even occur to her to lie.

"It is a cute nose." He looked appalled the moment the words had left his lips. His cheeks also turned a ruddy color.

"Thank you." Compliments should be accepted, especially since, in Chandra's world, they came few and far between. Her father didn't believe in sparing his brood from the truth, and her grandmother turned bluntness into an art. "May I?" She grabbed the stethoscope from a tray against the wall. It dangled from her hand, an old-fashioned method still used by so many. There was something about listening to the steady thump of a heart that connected a doctor to the patient.

"Must you?"

"It is why I am here."

He sat down on the bed. "I assure you I'm not dead," he said as he braced his hands on his thighs and kept his shoulders back.

She stepped in close enough to reach out and placed the diaphragm on his chest. Her fingers didn't touch him, the metal drum did, and yet, a sizzling sensation seemed to rise from his skin.

The thump of his heart beat rather fast. She slid the diaphragm over a little and leaned closer to him, as if proximity would change what she heard.

Thump. Thump. Thump. Thump.

It sounded normal, except... "Is that an echoing heartbeat I hear?" Her nose wrinkled as she looked at him.

"No idea what you're talking about. I'm as human as you."

Snort. "I doubt that. I'm going to check from your back."

"You think I trust you enough to get behind me?"

"Are you admitting you're scared of a girl half your size?"

She almost could have sworn she heard a voice say, *I am very ssscared because you make me feel thingsss...*

Perhaps there was something in the air making her imagine voices.

"All it takes is one knife in the back from someone you trust."

The softly spoken words had her pausing before placing the stethoscope on his skin. "Fear should not remove your ability to trust."

"Death doesn't give second chances."

"Aren't you Mr. Philosophy." She stopped hesitating and pressed the diaphragm against the skin of his back. A nice back showing yet again more signs of malnutrition with all his vertebrae and ribs standing out in stark relief. He didn't flinch or tense as she moved around for a listen to his lungs. He even took in a deep breath, which he used to speak.

"Philosophy can be a great guidance for life. I was raised in a household that relied on history and famous words. I pick and choose what calls to me."

"Sounds gentler than a fist."

His body tensed, all his muscles suddenly becoming rigid. "Someone hit you?" He sounded so aghast.

"Many times. My father called it discipline. I called it too many beers after work." Her father had been raised in a world that didn't believe in sparing the rod, especially with his daughters.

"Abuse of younglings is wrong."

"It is. And so is the abuse of people." She moved away from his back to where he could see her again. "If you're being held against your will, like me, then it's wrong."

"You're trying too hard to gain my trust. You're making it too obvious you're a plant by Parker."

"A plant?" Her eyes widened. "Are we back on that conspiracy theory again? I didn't think cannabis and other hallucinogens that cause paranoia were part of your drug roster."

"Why lie to him, Doctor Kashmir?" Parker's words purred from the speakers. "He's figured it out."

"Figured out what?" She didn't understand.

"The plan to have him trust you and reveal all his secrets. We gave it a good try. A shame it didn't work."

"You're lying." She could feel the panic bubbling in her as Parker strove to anger the man. He did it on purpose, and she couldn't help but recall the warning words of the guards who'd brought her to this room. "That never happened. I swear."

Her assertion only seemed to anger the patient. "We're done here." He stood again from the gurney and stepped on the fallen IV bag, causing the end of the tube to squirt brackish muck.

Poisonous-looking muck. A muck he thought she was party to.

"What are you doing?"

"I'm bored of this conversation." He stalked toward her, and she backed away, eyes wide, hand clutching at her neck. A neck he'd almost crushed before.

Hissing filled the air as Parker, or whoever kept an eye, released the security measure to ensure no outbreaks. She couldn't help but clap a hand over her mouth, utterly horrified. The threatening man before her might be able to handle the dosage, but she... "No. Too much of that stuff will kill me."

The gas tickled the inside of her nose. She tried to not respond, but in the end, she couldn't help but breathe, her hand over her nose and mouth providing a poor filter. Her knees buckled, but she never hit the floor. Hands caught her. A fuzzy masculine voice said, "I will avenge you."

Chapter Five

Anger chased him into wakefulness. Tomas couldn't at first remember why he was so enraged, but once he did, he growled.

Parker had killed the yummy-smelling doctor. It bothered him. He didn't understand why.

The woman had not suffered. The gas slipped her quickly into a deep sleep. She wouldn't have felt a thing.

Tomas did, though. Felt something for the death of a woman he barely knew.

I'm done with this place.

Jumping to his feet, he went straight from seeming slumber to full alertness. No more playing games.

He tugged on the chain tethering his left arm. Wound it around his bicep.

Before he could do anything further, Parker's voice emerged to taunt, in person as opposed to via a microphone. A peek upwards showed the man leaning over the railing of the pit. He, unfortunately, didn't fall in. "There's my sleeping beauty. Have a good nap?"

"The beast and I want to thank you for it, so stay right there. I'll be up in a minute." Tomas began to tug on the chain.

"Is someone feeling a little testy today?"

"You killed the woman." He couldn't stem his irritation over it.

"I did," Parker admitted. "But it was your fault. If you would just do as you're told, none of this would be necessary."

"None of this would have happened if I'd pulled your head off."

"Always with the futile threats. What a pity you're not strong enough to do anything about it. And speaking of strength, since you won't cooperate, perhaps I'll have better luck with someone else in your family."

The threat froze him. "Don't you go near them." He might not be close to them, but no one messed with his blood.

"You can't stop me. Just like you couldn't keep me from killing that woman today." Parker leaned over the railing, a speck at the top, but Tomas could clearly see him. "You're nothing. A weak and pathetic specimen of your kind. Almost no better than a human." No hiding the sneer.

Tomas yanked, hard enough that metal screamed and snapped.

"One," he counted. He wrapped the other side around his hand and yanked. *Crack*. "Two."

"Gas him," Parker ordered.

Tomas freed his legs, one by one, and from the vents in the wall only a small cloud puffed.

The fan circulating the air, usually no more than a hum, made a noise, a very unhealthy noise, and whirred to a stop.

"Containment measures activated," a robotic voice announced.

An alarm went off, one without sound, just a strobing light at the top of the pit. Parker's head lifted as he slapped the railing. "What happened to the distribution system?"

Another voice replied, out of sight, but not hearing. "I don't know, sir."

Parker's nostrils flared. "'I don't know' is not an answer. Fix it."

They'd better fix it quickly. Tomas dangled the loose chains. "Uh-oh, are you having problems in your Frankenstein-ish Utopia?"

Parker ignored Tomas, and Tomas didn't appreciate it one bit.

"I'm coming for you."

"Go ahead and try." Parker cast him a glance. "You'll fail like all the others. But just in case." Parker turned away. "Get rid of him."

Those were Parker's final words before he disappeared from sight and the ring around the pit found itself swarmed by guards.

When they lifted their guns to fire, Tomas smiled. "Don't miss."

Shadows suddenly dropped, extinguishing all light, all visibility.

Wild shots were fired, but it was the screaming that really lifted things up a notch.

Chapter Six

The sound of gunfire and the last rumble had stopped hours ago, and still, Chandra hesitated to come out of hiding. When the silent alarms had started, she did the only thing she could think of, what they'd taught in the lockdown practices at school—hide.

She'd not survived being gassed—and revived with an antidote—to die now because someone was trying to liberate the medical research lab. At least, she hoped it was liberation. She dreaded to think what it would mean if something worse than her patient had gotten loose.

But he'd claimed he was here alone.

He claimed. And what made her think she could trust his word? No matter what currently happened, the best thing to do was stay out of the way and survive.

The metal cabinet in her room proved easy to squeeze into, and she was glad of it because, when the gunfire stopped, something made the whole place rumble. Chunks of debris fell, hitting the floor hard. Things creaked and groaned, making her cringe. *Please don't let the ceiling fall on me.*

The shaking tapered, and yet she didn't move. In the cabinet, there was a measure of safety.

A sense of *nothing can get me here.*

Fear kept her hiding as she waited and waited to see if someone would come looking for her. Time passed. She thought she heard a step in the hall. Possibly imagined it.

More seconds on the clock ticked tirelessly along. Hiding was all well and good, except reality intruded. Eventually, her bladder reminded her that she couldn't stay here forever.

What felt like an eternity after the last discernible tremble, she unfolded herself from the cramped space and basically spilled onto the floor as her numb legs refused to cooperate. Lucky for her, the lab appeared empty and quiet. Too quiet.

Was anyone still alive? The fact that no one came looking didn't bode well.

Only heavy silence blanketed everything, reinforcing the sad truth that she was alone. Then again, she'd been almost entirely alone since her capture a few days ago. The guards certainly didn't socialize much, and she'd only briefly met a few other doctors before being sequestered again.

Are they alive and huddling in their rooms, too? Perhaps, she wasn't alone.

I'm not. She shouldn't forget who else shared this place.

The patient with the dark eyes that sparked with green fire—they didn't glow, not yet, but Chandra began to think he could be the man in the video.

How had the patient fared from the quake? Did he even live? He claimed to live in the pit.

How dangerous is he that they force him in there?

So dangerous, he hadn't killed her when he

had the chance.

Why didn't he kill me?

She'd had time to wonder about it during her time inside the cabinet. Time to wonder since her heart stopped racing from the neutralizing agent for the sleeping drug.

If Chandra didn't know better, she would have sworn at times the patient flirted with her. More disturbing, a part of her had responded to him.

Attracted to an alpha-hole. Her therapist had warned it might happen, despite Chandra's intense dislike of growing up with one as a father.

Yet, how had Marisol explained it? *"You'll date smart men. Men like you who use their brains, not their fists. You will think you are attracted."*

"I am," she'd agreed. *Her latest boyfriend was proof.*

"Yet you always crave something more. You'll want a man who can take charge."

In that, Marisol was wrong. Chandra preferred the lack of strife an omega male brought. She had no interest in men who thought highly of themselves or ordered women around. So why her intense attraction to the patient?

I can't keep calling him the patient. He had a name. She just didn't know it yet, and she might never know it if he didn't survive whatever had happened.

As she walked the hall, she noted the heaving floor tiles and the dipping ceiling. In some sections, parts of it hung down, and she skirted these, especially the innocuous dangling wires. If she hurt herself, who knew if or when anyone would find her. Maybe never.

She'd rarely seen anyone since her arrival. Most of her instructions—and threats—came via hidden speakers.

She'd heard nothing since the quake.

What did that mean?

Have we been abandoned?

It wouldn't surprise her. That seemed to be standard operation with illegal medical labs these days. Abandon ship before discovery. And if this medical research facility owned by Parker held true to pattern, he'd wipe all traces. Which meant this lab would disappear, along with anything and everyone in it.

I need to find a way out. But before that, she had to do the right thing, even if freeing *him* would probably result in him eating her in a single gulp.

She'd heard the rumors, read the reports. He was a killer.

A stone-cold killer of humans.

Yet, it didn't seem fair to let him slowly starve in his prison. Never mind she'd starve with him, too, if no one came to save her or she didn't find a way out.

She really wasn't counting on rescue. Who would come? No one but Parker and a few of the soldiers who worked on the outside even knew this lab existed, so she could only wonder who'd come to raid. Was it Dex? Had he done some geeky computer thing and managed to trace her location?

Hesitating at every step, Chandra exited her hallway, which held three labs and some sleeping quarters. According to Parker—who loved the sound of his own voice—this was where they sent the scientists who got too nosey in their other places of business.

At the moment, only Chandra and a few other doctors lived here. The guards stayed in a separate wing.

At the end of the long hall, loomed a door leading into the true belly of the hidden facility. She peered around the doorjamb to see another empty hall and more evidence of damage. The only sound was her feet in their thin slippers, slapping on the tile floor—a lovely gift from those who'd kidnapped her and brought her to this place. She didn't even get to wear her own clothes. Just nondescript smocks and pants, along with the long white coat that she insisted on wearing so she could remind herself of the oath she'd taken. An oath Parker wanted to twist.

The gentle hum of the air recirculation system uttered an occasional stutter, a gentle reminder that, once the power failed, she'd die from a lack of oxygen. This place didn't have any windows that she'd seen. Eventually, fresh air would become an issue, but it would be a gentle way to die. She'd just fall asleep and never wake.

At the end of the hall was a door that required a swipe of her keycard. It still had power for the moment, but she hesitated before entering.

She'd never gone in there before while he was awake, mostly out of fear. She'd watched the videos. Seen what he could do.

But who could blame him… She reminded herself that he hadn't killed her before when he had the chance.

Before she could change her mind, Chandra entered the musty space. A cave within a building, within a mountain. A prison for someone very dangerous, or so Parker claimed.

A balcony made of riveted metal plates ringed a deep pit, the stone walls of it sheer and glasslike, impossible to climb, not that the man chained at the bottom could move that far. As the guards had explained, the tethers binding the man were short. The drugs they injected him with strong. So very strong. And yet, those drugs would have worn off a few hours ago without someone to administer them.

Chandra peered down into the depths, noting the shadows. She knew from the video she'd seen just how well he could blend with the darkness.

Was that him? It had to be, because how many men could Parker have hiding in a hole?

Actually, given Parker's mental instability, it could be quite a few.

But, right now, she was only worried about one man. The man she'd seen only once before. The one who'd chosen not to kill her.

Did he hide below and watch? Did he plan her death?

Would he understand she was here to free him? *I'll get you out of there. Even if it's the last stupid thing I do.*

The security chamber, usually manned by guards, was empty—and not gently. There were bullet holes in the glass. Blood spatters on the floor and across the blank monitors. The screens with their views of the pit were dead, completely dead, along with many of the lights.

Sabotage or something more frightening?

Had systems already failed? Surely, there were backup generators. Or had those been destroyed in the attack? What if the engine running this place died? Then she'd be in the dark and unable to help him or herself.

Help me my goddess, Devi.

Help yourself. Funny how the reply sounded like her grandmother.

Back out in the parapet area, she eyed the pit. She saw no way down. No way to help the patient. She leaned over and peered more intently. She saw a strange heap at the bottom.

Was that a boot? Odd since the patient was usually kept barefoot.

If that wasn't him at the bottom, then… "Where are you?" she muttered.

"Looking for me?" The words were whispered in a gruff voice from behind, enough to startle Chandra into falling forward, into the pit!

Chapter Seven

Of all the clumsy things to do, she fell, and Tomas prepared to let gravity do its thing.

Totally should have. After all, why save a woman he thought already dead? Given his certainty, it was rather surprising to suddenly find her roaming around.

His bad really, as he'd never even thought to look for her. After he'd taken care of the guards—with glee he could not contain—he'd been busy sorting through the computers, trying to glean any information he could before he left this place.

He took too long playing with the guards. By the time he'd made it out of the pit area, a little scratched, plenty happy, and streaked in blood, Parker had already launched his wiping bomb. As in all the hard drives in this place appeared fried. Useless.

Such a waste. He spent a moment smashing things when he realized it.

Once he'd calmed, he was ready to go. Time to leave this place. And he would have, except she wandered into view. Alive.

Mine.

If she managed to live. Sigh. All that thinking took but a mere moment, and in that time, he lunged to grab her. He kept her from falling. He couldn't have said why.

Why did he not kill her like the others? She was a doctor, no better than the rest. Her status here mocked him with her pristine white coat.

Still, though, even if she was the enemy, she smelled yummy. Too delicious to splatter the bottom of the pit with.

As she teetered, he grabbed her by the shirt and yanked her to safety.

Breath emerging in short, hot pants, she leaned against the wall and regarded him with big eyes.

He crossed his arms over his bare chest and fixed her with a stare. "You're supposed to be dead."

"Funny, I was going to say the same thing of you."

The corner of his mouth lifted. "I'm not that easy to kill."

"So I see. You also don't look like you need rescuing." She sounded disgruntled by the fact.

"I never did." He'd just chosen to take his time.

"Then why didn't you leave before? Or did you like being tied down, drugged, and used as a guinea pig?"

"An unavoidable side effect of my decision to remain in captivity."

She blinked the longest, darkest lashes at him. "No one decides to be a prisoner."

"Why not? I wasn't doing anything truly that interesting. Once I realized Parker had an interest in my genes, I found myself interested, too."

"Did you find out what you wanted?"

His lips pulled down. "No. Which means these past few months were a waste of time." He'd accomplished nothing and would have to return empty-handed to his home. Not a single new treasure for his trove. He spun on his heel, his bare foot easily sliding on the simple tiled floor.

"Where are you going?"

"Out of here. Like I said, I'm done." Poor girl was hard of hearing, or stupid, which would be a shame. She was quite pretty.

And yummy smelling.

"I'm coming with you."

The light touch shouldn't have shocked him. The doctor had touched him before. Yet, after the intensely strange rage he'd gone through when he thought her dead, only to find out it was a sham, left him a tad volatile. He spun and roared.

Loudly.

Definitely not humanly.

"Don't. Touch. Me."

The brave façade she wore crumbled, and she reeled from him, hitting the wall, not using it for support; instead, choosing to slump until she sat on the ground.

He'd scared her.

It didn't make him feel as good as usual. As a matter of fact, he felt downright wretched about it. Especially since she stared with such fear.

"Don't look at me like that," he snapped. The warning didn't stop her.

From her spot on the floor, knees pulled to her chin, and her dark eyes wide, she stared at him, radiating terror. She wet her lips, the tip of a pink tongue that tempted.

I should kiss her.

Don't you mean kill her? He assumed a slip of his mental tongue.

"Who—who are you?" she asked, her voice quavering.

As if she didn't know. "You can stop pretending."

"I'm not pretending. I was only ever given a file, and while it went into detail about your vital statistics, nothing mentioned your name. Who are you?"

"Don't you mean what am I?" He laughed. "Did Parker seriously not tell you?"

"Parker doesn't tell anyone anything. And I only realized after my capture that I was working for him. Before here, I was a scientist for Lytropia. Or, as it turns out, a subsidiary arm of Bittech."

"Never heard of either." He shrugged.

"How could you never hear of them? Bittech is the medical institute where Parker made his announcement."

"What announcement?"

"The one telling the world about his kind."

"Ah, yes, I vaguely recall him droning on and on about his enlightenment of the world in regards to shifters. Can't say as I paid much attention, what with him being beneath me and all." The day-to-day lives of the animals on the planet didn't usually concern him much.

"Who are you?" she asked him again.

"Humans." Said with a long-suffering sigh. "You have such an irritating way of constantly nagging until you get answers. You may call me

Tomas, since you insist."

"Introducing yourself is called common courtesy."

"And yet you've yet to introduce yourself. I know you only as Doctor Kashmir."

"That is my name."

"Not your first name."

"Chandra."

"Chandra," he repeated. Rolling it on his tongue. Finding it to his liking. Exotic, like her.

She would make a nice addition to his collection.

No, not for the collection. Tomas didn't deal in people. Ever. Not even attractive female ones.

A slight tremor suddenly rocked the installation. Rock cracked, and dust sifted. The unrelenting groan of metal twisting didn't reassure.

I think I broke the place. He might have gotten a little violent during his liberation—in other words, knocked a few important support beams out of place. "I think it's time we made our departure."

"We? Does this mean I can come with you?" Her voice lifted in an optimistic lilt.

"For now. I'd hate to have to listen to your complaining or screams if I left you behind."

"Your generosity overwhelms."

"It should. I'm not a man who gives often." Tomas usually preferred to share nothing. So this helping-hand thing seemed out of character.

Why was he acting like this?

Because I know I can use her to find out more about Parker and his plans.

Make her talk even if she claimed she knew nothing. Apply a little torture, the oral kind with lots of tongue.

"Thank you for helping me."

"Don't thank me." He definitely had an ulterior motive. "I am not your patient anymore, doctor. As a matter of fact, I'd say the drastic reversal in roles means you should pretty much do or say anything I want."

"What do you want?" How breathless she sounded.

"You."

Gasp.

And then, as if he'd orchestrated the moment, the lights went out. Cool. *Let the fun begin.*

Chapter Eight

"Did you seriously say let the fun begin?" Incredulity marked Chandra's tone. "That is so not right." Not when darkness pressed in on all sides in a suffocating layer.

"Do you not see the fun in our situation?"

"It's dark."

"I know. It's perfect. Before, you could see the depressing lack of opposition around us. There was nothing to really fear."

"Exactly. That was a good thing. Now I can't see anything." Which meant she was alone in the dark with Tomas. Tomas and nothing else. There wasn't any sound in the darkness. She didn't even hear herself as she held her breath to listen.

Dear, Devi. Save me.

His voice, where it tickled across her lobe in a warm puff, sent a shiver down her spine. "The darkness is a friend. It can surround and comfort you. The dark can be a shield against the light."

The reply caused her to blink. "Either that was poetry, or you are truly insane." Very possible given his captivity. And she was alone with him!

"Your heart is racing." His voice purred around her. "Pittering and pattering. You're so frightened, and yet you don't beg for your life."

At his taunting words, her back straightened. As she jabbed her elbow back, she was rewarded with hard abs. But it still gave her some satisfaction to hit him as she stated, "Your bullying tactics don't scare me. If you were going to kill me, you'd have done it by now and tossed me into the hole with the rest." Because she suspected the heap at the bottom of the pit, featuring boots, was why she hadn't seen any guards or staff once she left her room.

"Killing you would be such a waste, though." He drew near. She could feel heat radiating from him in a wave. "It's been a long time since I was with a woman."

The threat caused a frisson, less of fear and more of excitement. What was it about this man that appealed to her more carnal nature?

She steeled herself against him. "Your lack of coitus is going to be even longer than that if you don't shower the next time before making bold attempts at seduction."

For a moment, silence. Then a querying, "Did you just say I smell?"

Not really. For a man living in a hole, he seemed remarkably clean—if she ignored the blood. Still, though, a girl should have standards. "Even you have to admit you could use a bit of R & R. Maybe get a shave and a haircut to straighten things out. Antiperspirant is everyone's friend." She blabbed, wondering why she couldn't shut up. *I need to shut up.* But no, she kept going. "And the whole barefoot in scrubs look. It's gotta go."

"If I strip the offending clothing, will you join me?"

The bold question stole her next words. He

wasn't seriously suggesting they...

Rumble. The slight tremor reminded her of where they were. Their little bubble wasn't impermeable to calamity. As fascinating as she found talking to Tomas, she had to remember they were in danger. At least, she was. Tomas seemed quite capable of caring for himself now that he'd escaped his chains.

"We shall continue this conversation when we've reached a better locale," he said. "Preferably one with a shower to please the doctor."

"How are we supposed to find our way out?" She hated how her voice quavered. Sure, things seemed dire at the moment. Standing around in the pitch black inside a top-secret and secure installation wasn't exactly ideal.

You forgot the part where you're with a known killer.

Who wanted to see her naked. Be still her racing heart.

"Follow me."

At that, she blew out a breath. "Exactly how am I supposed to follow? I can't even see you."

"At all?"

"Would I be asking if I could? Not all of us have night vision. We need to find a flashlight or something. The thing is, I have no idea where they'd keep one."

He made a noise. "We don't need a flashlight. Just hold on to me."

Fingers, hot and callused, gripped hers and pressed them against fabric. She linked her fingers into the waistband of his pants and couldn't help a sharp awareness of him.

"I've got you." She did, but it didn't prove very useful. It was still dark.

Tomas moved with a long stride, and she took two to keep up. And when he stopped? She bounced off him.

Twice.

The third time, he whirled and caught her. It brought her flush against his chest.

"Are you this clumsy as a doctor, too?" he asked.

"Maybe if you were a little more considerate instead of dragging and abruptly stopping."

"Are you blaming the innocent one in all this for your ineptness?" The fine snobbery in his query made it sound so elegant.

"You're the one with size, what, fourteen, maybe fifteen feet?" Women noticed things like hands and feet on a man. The matrons in her family tended to start all discussions about potential bachelors with an observation of fertility.

"I am perfectly proportioned to my height."

"Which is also really tall." So tall, she felt rather short.

"You make it sound negative. I thought women liked tall men."

"We like men a few inches taller than us. A girl would need a stepstool just to reach you."

"No need to stand on anything. I am capable of solving a height difference."

Before Chandra realized what he meant to do, her feet left the floor, and she was lifted, hoisted high enough that firm lips pressed against hers. She sucked in a startled breath.

He laughed softly against her mouth. "See?

Height is no issue."

"Apparently, boundaries are. I never said you could kiss me."

"That wasn't a kiss." The words vibrated against her lower lip. "This is."

He meshed his mouth to hers, immediately teasing and massaging her lips, pulling at the lower one for a suck. She should have pushed him away.

After all, he took rather than asked. However, she would be hard-pressed to deny she wanted it. The kiss ignited all her senses. It shouldn't have. She didn't know this man, and what she knew was disturbing.

The kiss didn't care about any of those things.

Her arms wound around his neck as his fingers dug into her waist, holding her aloft. She lost herself in the moment until his mocking words broke the spell.

"Will you still claim I can't have you?"

She bit him.

He cursed and set her down abruptly. "That was uncalled for."

"Next time, keep your brute strength to yourself."

"How about I keep everything to myself. Find your own way out."

The implication horrified. He was going to leave her alone in the dark! She desperately wanted to scream—*don't leave me*. Inside, a part of her whimpered in fear. However, Chandra was not about to ask him for help. Let him selfishly leave. She didn't need him.

I'll find my own way out.

She felt around with her fingers in front of her, using tiny, shuffling steps as she cast about blindly.

Shuffle. Wave the hands. More shuffling. Flailing widely.

A heavy sigh filled the silence. Not by her.

"Are you criticizing me?" she asked, quite annoyed.

"More like cringing at your lack of skills when it comes to survival."

"They didn't teach me how to escape a hidden lab with no power in school. If you don't like it, then leave. No one's making you watch."

Another heavy sigh. "That's just it. I want to leave, and yet I can't. Not when you're so obviously incompetent. You'll die of old age at the rate you're moving."

"At least I'll live to a ripe old age," she muttered. Then squeaked as she found herself lifted, princess style this time, with his arms looped under her knees and back.

"Try something novel and be quiet now while I get us out of here."

Since getting out of the dark really worked for her, Chandra sealed her lips. She still couldn't quite figure out how it was she turned into a chatterbox of inanities around him. Perhaps he oozed some kind of pheromone that rendered her stupid. Who knew what he could do, especially given Parker's experiments.

I can fly, but that'sss not becaussse of Parker.

The alien words, with a hint of a lisp, floated into her mind, and she almost shrieked.

"Who said that?" she exclaimed out loud.

"Said what?" he asked.

"Someone just said they could fly." She paused. "In my head."

"You're mistaken."

"I am not mistaken. I heard someone talking. Dear, Devi." She moaned. "I'm hearing disembodied voices. This is bad. So bad."

"Insanity is treatable."

"Maybe if my family believed in modern medicine. If my grandmother finds out, I'll probably have to go through an exorcism." Poor cousin Juliette. She still had a haunted look in her eye from her intervention, but as *daadee* had confided to Chandra, "At least she finally stopped running around with those boys." Loose morals weren't tolerated in the family.

"You're not haunted. And that voice won't be talking to you again. Promise."

"So, it was your fault. You're like some kind of psychic. That's why you're here, why Parker captured you. Are you reading my mind right now?" Despite knowing the futility, she let go of his neck to cover her ears, lest he discover how much she enjoyed being carried in his arms. Chandra wasn't a girl with a lot of experience when it came to the opposite sex, the whole, no-boys-until-marriage thing being drilled into her from birth.

"Don't be ridiculous. I do not read minds. I can just sometimes speak to a select few."

"Just because you can doesn't mean you should."

"I would be glad to stop talking entirely."

"Fine."

He didn't reply.

And despite the fact that she should have expected it, she sniffed. Jerk. A jerk who was kindly taking her out of this place. Easily, too.

"Is it me, or are the doors all unlocked?" Unusual. Chandra would have guessed everything went into lockdown in case of a power failure.

"The passages are open because I might have gone exploring earlier."

"And you didn't leave?"

"I was looking for survivors."

"Do you know who attacked the lab?"

"Is this a trick question? I'm the one who cleaned out this place. I just wished I'd done it quicker. I missed Parker."

Did Tomas mean to imply that he'd killed everyone? She swallowed hard. "Why kill everyone?"

"Because they offended me. I warned them to get out of my way. They didn't listen, which was really their own fault since they know I'm not a man to exaggerate."

"Are you going to get rid of me, too?"

"I might if you don't stop asking questions."

She tried silence for a moment, but with the darkness so oppressive, and his body so close to hers, she couldn't think straight. She couldn't think at all.

"Where are we?"

"Must be a record. You lasted a whole ninety seconds that time."

His condescending tone stung. "Maybe I wouldn't ask so many questions if you'd answer me. Everything you say is couched in grand words and threats. Why can't you speak plainly?"

"Are you accusing me of being a snob?"

"Yes."

"Then you'd be right."

"You should add jerk to that, too," she muttered.

"What's that? You want me to leave you here? In the dark?"

She wrapped her arms so tightly around his neck, it would take the Jaws of Life to pry her away.

"I'll take that as a no."

"Don't you dare leave me here."

"Or what?"

"I'll have my grandmother curse you."

"I'm so scared."

"You should be. Uncle Sanji hasn't been able to cheat on Aunt Selma since my *daadee* cursed him with impotence."

"I have no plans to meet your family, so your threat means nothing."

He made a good point, so why could she so easily see herself presenting Tomas to her *daadee* for her approval?

"The door leading outside is right through here," Tomas remarked.

She didn't need him to tell her that because she could see the hints of daylight creeping around the edges of the door. It illuminated the room in a shadowy pallor that showed off an unexpected grouping of machinery and tools.

She pushed at his chest, and he set her down. "Is it me, or does this look like the inside of a shed?" Definitely not the building she'd expected to emerge in.

"It is a shed. Great camouflage, actually.

This cabinet"—he rapped on the metal frame—
"hides the door leading inside the mountain."

"Which mountain, though? I don't recall
any big enough near the Lytropia Institute."

"I don't know what institute you're referring
to. I'm not sure where we are. I was kidnapped
while on an archeological dig in Sudan. I assumed
I'd been brought back to the States. I just don't
know where."

"You're an archeologist?"

"Don't sound so shocked. I happen to be
quite renowned in my field. Was tenured at a
prestigious university, too, before my capture. I've
even written for several magazines about my
findings."

"I can't believe you're a scholar. You do
realize you're throwing the shoe size schematic off."
Grandmother would find this intriguing, as would
Chandra's aunts.

"I don't think I want to know what that
means."

And he never would, because Tomas, for all
her attraction to him, wasn't someone she'd
introduce to her family. Chandra wasn't ever getting
married. Again. Not after the fiasco she'd endured
with Ishaan.

Arranged marriages were only beneficial to
the parents. The poor victims of them could usually
barely tolerate each other. At least, that was the case
with her and Ishaan. He resented her so badly.
Especially since the marriage was meant to cover
his shame. His parents were very upset by certain
choices he'd made.

Chandra wasn't about to make another

mistake with Tomas.

Freedom beckoned. The daylight creeping through cracks teased, and she moved to the door excitedly.

"Thank you for finding the way out. How far do you think we'll have to go to find civilization?" She put her hand on the knob—

"Don't go out there," he shouted as he lunged.

—and the door swung open, and she faced someone in a dark mask holding a gun. A gun pointed in her direction.

The guy dressed in combat gear fired, and searing pain engulfed her as something impacted her body. She hit the ground with a startled gasp. Couldn't quite blink away her shock.

Pain set in.

Darkness tore at her as more sharp retorts echoed all around.

She faded. Faded into the darkness.

...until light tore it away.

The stabbing brilliance against her eyelids forced her to wedge them open. They felt so heavy. All of her felt heavy. Especially her arms and legs. They wouldn't move at all when she tugged at them.

On account of me being tied down!

Chapter Nine

"Help!"

The doctor shrieked, and a moment later, he clapped a hand over her mouth. It didn't stop her attempts to scream.

"Shhh," he whispered as he kept her voice muffled. "You have to be quiet."

Wide eyes, the depths a drowning pool of chocolate, stared fearfully at him.

It bothered Tomas. *She shouldn't fear me. I've done nothing to harm her.* On the contrary, he'd saved her. She should be thanking and rewarding him.

However, she didn't seem to recognize that and persisted in casting him a terrified gaze.

"Stop the histrionics. I'm not going to hurt you. If I let you go, will you promise not to scream?" Such a cliché thing to ask, and yet, it imparted some measure of ease to her.

She nodded.

"I mean it. No yelling. We're not safe here." Nowhere in the area was safe, although the patrols were thinning.

Tomas should have left the area once he dispatched the soldiers who'd returned to complete the destruction of the hidden laboratory. However, someone messed up those plans.

Chandra had gotten shot, and well...he might have gone off on a rampage. He hoped it wouldn't become a trend, especially as it only seemed to happen because of her.

"Mggshad." Her attempt to speak vibrated against the palm of his hand. He'd prefer her mouth vibrating on another part of him.

I wonder if she talks during sex.

Now was not the time to find out.

"No screaming. I mean it." He removed his hand.

She didn't yell, but she spoke quite firmly. "Untie me at once." Her demand might have proven more imperious without the reedy thread of fear running through her tone.

"Why would I untie you? I don't recall you untying me when the roles were reversed."

"I never had a chance. You broke out of the bonds."

"True. I did." He couldn't help but smile. "Very well. You may do the same." He leaned away from the bed and rested his hip against the bulky dresser crowding his back.

"You know I can't get loose."

"How can you know that when you haven't even tried?" He teased her, another strange thing he did with Chandra.

"You're an arrogant ass." She didn't temper her words, and she invoked a few choice ones in another language. At least, he assumed she cursed. It sounded rather melodic to him.

She tugged and pulled, her face turning red, enough that he feared the strain pulling open her wound.

"You're going to hurt yourself," he chided. As for the reason she'd gotten hurt? His fault because he'd let her go out the door first. An error on his part. His earlier sweep of the area had shown no signs of recent passage outside the shed door.

But he'd fucked up. She went out the door first and got hit with a bullet meant for him.

She tossed him a glare through the dark hank of hair that fell over her eyes. "I'm going to hurt you if you don't set me free."

"That seems like an oxymoronic statement given you can't hurt me so long as you're confined."

"Let me go," she yelled, quite losing control. It made her only more attractive. The cool doctor losing it. Her cheeks taking on a flush, her eyes bright with fury. Much better than the dull shine of fever and a thousand times better than death. She was so fragile.

I must keep her safe.

The very concept proved novel. Since when did he care about keeping people, especially a human, safe? The only time he usually did it was as part of his job, mostly because the paperwork when a colleague or student got killed on a jobsite in a foreign country was a right pain to deal with. Given his preference for solitude, he stayed away from family. There were less emotional entanglements that way. And as for women…women were there to sate a need, not keep around.

He chose to resort to familiar arrogance to ensure she didn't guess the turmoil he felt toward her. "Instead of yelling at me, you should be thanking me. I saved your life. I could have left you to your fate. But no, I lowered myself to help you.

Really, humans nowadays have no sense when it comes to proper manners."

"Don't you throw manners at me. You are old enough to know that you can't keep women prisoner and say it's for their own good."

"Prisoner?" He stood away from the desk and loomed over her. "I saved you. Or have you forgotten you were shot? I'll admit leaving you to die was my initial impulse, but then this strange thing nagged me into lugging your ungrateful body to safety."

"You mean a thing like a conscience."

"Is that what it was?" He frowned. "I didn't think I owned one of those."

"Well, lucky you. You have one. And you saved me. Thank you." Added begrudgingly. "Now, will you please untie me?"

"If you insist, and only because you remembered your manners."

"I didn't see you remembering your manners when the roles were reversed," she grumbled, rubbing her freed wrists.

"Because I was not in the mood to be gentlemanly. I reserve that aspect of myself for people I respect."

Her expression pinched. "Is this your subtle way of insulting me?"

"You seemed perfectly fine doing the same to me." In the darkness, during that small bubble of time, she'd spoken unafraid and, at times, brilliantly challenging. The kiss he took might have ignited his arousal, but it was the talking that fired his covetous soul.

"That was different, and don't ask me to

explain," she grumbled, "because I can't."

"You are such a fascinating mix, doctor. It's making it hard for me to decide how to classify you."

"Why class me at all?"

"Because that is how to decide a thing's worth."

"And is a thing's worth that important to you?"

"Anything that can be a treasure is." The sum of his life, and those of his kind, was based on the worth of their collection.

"People aren't treasures."

"Untrue. People can indeed be priceless and coveted."

"Let me guess, like Helen of Troy."

"Actually, she didn't exist, and the woman the legend was loosely based on wasn't that pretty. But you misunderstand. Relationships can be prized. And the closer the relationship, the more priceless it is." He could see he'd lost her. Anyone without a collection didn't understand how to place value. "Suffice it to say, people have varying worth."

"I think setting a price is barbaric and outdated, like arranged marriages."

"On that, we can agree." His kind had a thing about prearranging alliances. To strengthen the blood and ties between families was the excuse. It was cold and impersonal. Also entirely unwanted, yet another reason Tomas had severed himself from his Sept and gone rogue.

I will allow no one to dictate my fate.

But what if fate didn't play fair? His gaze

couldn't seem to move from Chandra. Her features were pale, her eyes marked with dark circles despite her extended repose.

She moved to sit up, and he quickly offered assistance. Even with his hands lifting and holding, she groaned. "Put me back down." He lowered her, and she glared at him. "What did you do to me? Why am I so dizzy? And why does my side hurt so badly?"

"I told you I had to drag you to safety." More like carried, but he didn't want to give the impression he mollycoddled. His grandmother had taught him women were just as strong as men, just more subtle about it.

"How long was I asleep?"

"Just over a day."

"A day?" She sat up again, and he caught her when she would have flopped over. It wasn't his brightest move, as it brought her into close proximity. Very close.

She didn't move away.

Neither did he. He might have held his breath when she leaned her head against his chest.

His heart fluttered. Probably a remaining issue with the drugs still leaching from his system.

"You mean to say you've been taking care of me all this time?" Again, quite incredulous.

When she said it like that, it sounded so emasculating. "You slept most of the time, so I spent a lot of time out and about, hunting." Probably a good thing she didn't ask what he chased. He got the impression she could be squeamish.

"Where are we?" she asked.

"Cabin in the foothills of the Rockies."

"Rockies? Impossible."

Again, she tried to rise and winced. He caught her and cradled her against his chest. She felt good there.

She belongsss with me, the dragon part of him chimed in.

"We can't be in the Rockies because when I encountered those *raakhas* on the road—"

"What's a rack-ass?" he asked.

"A demon with claws and teeth and wings. They chased me out of my car, and I ran to the building that isn't supposed to be there where there was the naked man."

He immediately stiffened. "What naked man?" His blood coursed hot.

"I don't know his name. I met him at that place that didn't exist. Some kind of military-like establishment but with no insignia. But that was in Idaho. I am supposed to be there. Not here." She rambled, her thoughts not fully coherent but still painting a picture.

Parker had transported her, and far? Why? What made her special? "You're definitely not in Idaho anymore."

"So you claim."

"So I know."

"But I don't want to be here." She said it almost petulantly.

"Too bad. You're going to have to get used to cool mountain springs, crisp, clean air, and pine needles." The only real scent he could say felt like home.

The fact that they were in the Rockies

worked better than great. It was a stroke of fucking luck. Tomas knew this place. He especially knew it well on the Canadian side. What he didn't understand was how his American cousins could allow something like Parker's illegal lab to flourish on their land, because he knew the people who lived around here. People like him.

Traitors.

He didn't know that for sure, but the mere fact that something Parker owned existed anywhere close to the mountains didn't look good for his brethren.

Still cradled against him, Chandra asked softly, "Are we in danger here?"

"Yes. There are forces in the woods looking for us." He didn't sugarcoat the delightful truth.

"Is it Parker?"

"Indirectly, yes. It's his men, sent to clean the area. They are aware that I escaped and are quite determined I not make it out of these mountains alive."

"So that's why you're still here? You're stuck?"

"Not one bit. I can leave anytime."

"Then why didn't you?"

Because he worried she wouldn't survive the flight. "I thought we could use a vacation."

"We?" Her gaze narrowed. "You stayed because of me, didn't you?" Said almost with accusation.

He made sure to look the height of nonchalance as he said, "Maybe. But don't read anything into it. I have need of you. Just my luck you humans have weak constitutions."

"Humans? Why do you say it in such a sneering way?"

Best he made things clear now. "Because you're a lesser species. Not your fault," he hastened to add. "But still true."

She didn't nod in agreement. She refused to see the truth. "What are you? What makes you better than me?"

"I don't think we have the time to list my innumerable qualities."

She shook her head. "You're an ass."

"An ass?" He arched a brow. "I've killed people for less."

"How nice that you kill to make yourself feel better. Sounds like a guy with self-esteem issues, which usually stem from feelings of inadequacy because of a smaller-than-normal sexual stature."

He blinked and laughed. "Oh, doctor, that would only be a burn if I didn't know the truth. I'd be happy to show you my stature."

"You're a pig." She said it, and yet, she remained cradled against him, trading insults. Did she grin like a fool during their exchange? Tomas had just realized he did. He knew she wasn't being insulting to be mean, but teasing him.

Flirting.

He could flirt back. "I am much more majestic than a porcine creature."

"Is majestic the clue? You're a lion."

"A mangy feline constantly hacking up hairballs?" He almost shuddered. "That hurts."

She giggled against his skin.

He could have taken her then and there.

"What are you?" Chandra asked.

He leaned back that he might better see her expression. "Take a guess."

She stared at him a moment. He waited for her to finally admit she knew what he was. To stop playing this game. Surely, she had to know. Parker hadn't dragged her across the country and kept her prisoner with Tomas to not tell her anything.

Parker was using Chandra, and Tomas hated that she wouldn't admit it. She lied to him. Everyone lied to him.

It's why it's better to not care about people, because they'll always hurt you.

A line creased her brow as she studied him. "I am not sure what you are. I can see you're different. There's something about you that feels very primal."

"Because I come from the oldest race on this planet." None of the others came close. Not even the long-lived faerie.

"Why not just tell me what you are?"

"Shall we play charades?"

Her lips twitched. She snickered.

He had to ask. "What's so funny?"

"Was thinking wouldn't it be funny if you were a duck. And then I pictured it."

It took him but a moment to feel affronted. How dare she imagine him as a noisy fowl he liked to eat—roasted with a mandarin sauce. Then he couldn't help but picture it and almost laughed himself. "I hate to disappoint, but while I do have wings and fly, I am not a duck."

"I guess it's not very majestic." Her eyes widened, and her lips stretched into a huge grin. "I know what you are, a swan king."

"No."

"Bear, on account of your grumpiness."

"No! Bears don't fly."

"I guess if you've got wings you're not some kind of fish."

No, he wasn't, but he felt an urge to drown himself in a lake.

"You can stop pretending ignorance." He shook his head. "I know Parker must have told you what I am and why he was holding me." Tomas couldn't keep listening to her lie.

"I am not pretending. I have no idea what you are and that short video I saw didn't really show much other than glowing green eyes."

"It also wasn't me." Because he'd never transformed, not even partially while in captivity.

Not that I remember. The very idea that he might have chilled him to the bone. *What did they do to me?*

"Are you sure it wasn't you? Because the video clip I saw showed the camera dropping down a shaft. Didn't you say they kept you in a pit?"

"You know they did, so stop playing innocent."

"I *am* innocent, so you need to stop being so suspicious. The entire reason I'm here is because I had some misguided idea about rescuing whoever was in that video."

"You? Rescue me?" He snorted.

"Yeah, not my brightest idea. Perhaps I am as stupid as my father claims."

"He calls you stupid?" Tomas might have to pay that man a visit.

"My father's lack of ability to recognize what

I've accomplished is not the issue here. Your stubbornness is. I'm a prisoner just like you."

"Prisoners don't work for Parker."

"I am not working for Parker. Well, I was, but not knowingly."

"You were one of his doctors."

"Yes, but I thought I was working for a legit company, and I will add that I never experimented with real people."

"Do you consider me a real person?"

Her nose wrinkled. "What else would you be?"

I could be yours. Thankfully, he didn't say that aloud. He would have to kill her for sure.

The more they spoke, the more she seemed to recover. He noted how clear her gaze seemed. Already, some of her pallor had receded as she returned to life.

"How does your wound feel? I should check it."

"You mean I didn't dream it? I was shot?" Her eyes widened in shock. "But I survived. How did you do that?" Her brow knit. "And why doesn't it hurt more?" She palpated the wound, her fingers pressing over the bandage. He'd raided the institute before it collapsed for supplies.

"I might have used an ancient remedy passed down in my family to help speed the healing of wounds." He was also perfectly posed to provide the most important ingredient.

"A family recipe?" Her eyes brightened. "I did a dissertation on folk medicine when I was in university. It's truly amazing some of the natural options available that aren't being better pursued for viability."

"You know, most women," he noted as he eased her back onto the bed, "would be more concerned about their wound. Will it scar? How bad is it?"

"I was shot. Of course I'll have a scar. As to how bad it is, I'm alive." She smiled. "Sometimes, it's a matter of looking at it the right way."

"Your positive attitude is downright baffling." His fingers tugged gently at the bandage he'd created to go over the paste. Lifting the gauze, he gently wiped at the discolored residue, revealing skin, knitted shut but still quite red and angry.

She craned her chin to see it and marveled. "Only a day old and look at it. You'd think more than a week had gone by. That's amazing."

"It is."

"So why haven't you patented the formula and made billions from it?"

Because his blood was the main ingredient, and there was only one of him.

"It's not a family secret if I share it with the world," he said, grabbing the plastic bag with the last bit of paste. He smeared it on. "And I have enough money."

"But think of how much it could help everyone."

"Not everyone should be helped." He pressed a piece of gauze against the smeared remedy. A few strips of tape held it in place.

"How soon before I can get out of this bed?"

"Now that you're awake, and the wound is closed, we can leave anytime you deem fit." He helped her sit.

She swung her legs over the edge of the bed. "Then how about now. I can walk if it means getting out of here before some of Parker's men find this cabin."

A few already had. He'd taken care of them.

"Walk out?" He chuckled. "Silly, doctor. I don't walk unless I have to. And even if I did, you're in no shape. You're still much too weak." But he knew what he should do to make her stronger.

"Where are you going?" she asked.

"To get you some food. I'm sure you're famished."

As if reminded, her stomach rumbled, and he was intrigued to notice her cheeks turned pink.

As it turned out, she was famished, but he wouldn't let her eat quickly, cautioning her to take small bites of the canned stew he'd found in a cupboard.

The hunting cabin proved well stocked with canned goods. It even had a pump for water.

Meal finished, her eyes drooped. "I'm so tired."

"All that chewing. I can see how it would be daunting."

"Are you always this snarky?"

"Do you have to make everything a question?"

"Yes." She went to sleep mid-smile, and he spent a moment staring at her.

She was so dangerous to be around.

I should leave.

He stuck close.

Next time she woke, light still flooded the room, the rays of it weaker as the freshness of morning had faded into end of day. Stopping in the doorway, he watched as she stretched. The paste must have solved any lingering soreness because she stretched both her arms and legs.

She noticed him. Her eyes widened, and her lips pulled into a welcoming smile. A smile for him.

He wanted to kiss that smile.

"Nice outfit," she said.

He looked down at his ensemble and could understand her mirth. Gone were the hospital garments, somewhat bedraggled from his altercations. Returning to the lab to raid it after his first medical supply run had proved a waste of time, as the installation was gone, a cave-in blocking the entrance. He'd need heavy machinery to get anywhere inside.

But he didn't need the hidden lab. The cabin he'd found, rustic and blending into the forest, provided an unexpected bonus. The plywood cabinets held some canned goods. A sectioned-off room had a bed—with a lumpy mattress—and dusty linens. The cabin even had water he could pump from a well and, nestled inside a trunk with mothballs, clothes. Not great clothes, but better than finding a large leaf for his man parts.

Currently, Tomas wore an ill-fitting T-shirt with a cartoon of a falling tree and the caption of "When a tree falls in the forest, get the chainsaw" and sweatpants that were way too short.

"I thought it rather vintage and stylish. Wait until you see the tee I have for you."

"I can't wait." She pointed. "Is that food for

me?"

Ah, yes, his reason for coming to see Chandra in the first place. He handed her a bowl with a spoon, more of the hearty canned stew, which she ate with gusto, fidgeting only at the end, probably because he couldn't stop staring.

Why did she fascinate him so much?

"You seem to be feeling better." And by feeling better, he meant remaining conscious. He'd spent a harrowing time wondering if she'd live or die. He'd done things he'd sworn to never do—like endanger himself, worry, and protect—for her.

"Much better, especially since I didn't nap a whole day straight this time."

"That's what you think."

"How long did I sleep?"

He laughed as her mouth rounded. "Only a few hours."

She shook her spoon at him. "You're bad."

"The baddest." He winked.

Him. Mr. Cool and Collected. Winked.

She blushed. It kind of made the emasculation worthwhile. What he didn't understand was how his mouth suddenly ended up against hers.

Not for long. A brief touch, just enough to ignite him. He drew back before it could go any further.

"Why did you stop?" He could tell by her horrified expression that she'd not meant to say that.

"I shouldn't have done it." He still didn't understand why he'd acted.

Sure you do, for the same reason you didn't leave

her behind to die.

"You regret kissing me?" Her lips turned down.

"It should have never happened."

"Why?"

"Because you're not my type."

Her head snapped back as if he'd struck her. In a sense, he had.

He waited for her counterattack. She didn't disappoint.

"I was your type when you lifted me in the institute and smothered me."

"I did not smother you. I was proving a point."

"And what were you proving this time?"

Apparently, that his attraction to her hadn't evaporated yet. "Why do you care why I kissed you?"

"Because men always have an ulterior motive. You're planning to use me somehow."

The accusation bothered, especially since he was still pretty sure she was out to use him. "Why are you making a big deal about the fact that I wanted to kiss you? You're an attractive woman." *Mine.*

"I am not yours."

Speaking aloud again. He'd have to find a way to curb his wayward self. "At the moment, you are my responsibility."

Her eyes widened. "And let me guess. Because I'm your supposed responsibility, you think you have the right to manhandle me anytime you like? Do you really think that gives you the right to do whatever you like to me?"

He got the impression that saying yes might not go over well. "A simple kiss of thanks would have been nice."

Her expression narrowed, and her lips pursed. "I don't owe you anything. I didn't ask you to take care of me."

"You could still thank me." Yes, he saw the hole he dug, but he just couldn't help himself. In his mind, he expected her to put out a little. Tomas wasn't used to having to chase women for action. They usually threw themselves at him.

"Thank you for doing a basic, humane thing."

"Not human."

"Fine, compassionate. Is that allowed?"

In his culture? Not all the time. Circumstances often played a part in whether someone got to live or die.

He took the empty bowl from her and placed it on the dresser. "Shall I help you dress?" That sounded better than arguing about his emasculating need to cater to one little caramel-skinned human.

She jabbed a finger in his directions. "Oh, no you don't. I know that look. That look doesn't say let me platonically get you into some clothes."

She was right. He'd prefer her out of them.

"What does my look say?" He'd gladly reward her if she guessed right.

"You're thinking of sex." Her nose wrinkled. "Is that all men think about?"

"At the moment? Yes." He couldn't admit it because that would emasculate him, but at the moment, Chandra consumed his thoughts. He'd spent the better part of the last day and a half watching her. Showing patience he didn't usually enjoy. He'd found himself fraught with worry when he'd gone on patrol. He didn't even enjoy victory when he'd eliminated a team of searchers. He worried he'd return to the cabin and find her gone.

For some reason, the idea of her not being around bothered him.

She can't leave.

"How can you lust after someone who's lain in bed for almost two days, who probably smells like a locker room, and who hasn't seen a toothbrush in days?"

"I cared for you. You're clean." The hardest chore he'd ever undertaken.

"You touched me?"

He nodded. And he'd not even copped a single inappropriate grope. His honor was shiny—his balls very blue.

She licked her lips. "Thank you." Her large eyes regarded him, and he couldn't resist. He leaned in for a kiss.

Another kiss from her sweet lips.

One he didn't ask for. Asking was for the weak. He took.

At least, Tomas *meant* to take and be the one in charge, except her hands clasped his cheeks, and before he could touch his mouth to hers, she took his with a hunger that froze him.

Lips flavored with beef stew and seasoning, along with her spice, teased him. The tip of her tongue slayed him. The soft moan as he cradled her body in his arms and pulled her close undid him.

She melted against him for just a moment

before she bit him!

"Ouch." He pulled away and glared.

She smirked. "Oops." It didn't sound repentant. "Much fun as this is, I need a bathroom."

Good, because he needed time to compose himself. Chandra kept throwing him off balance. She didn't act as she should.

And how is she supposed to act?

Pliant and willing? Then she'd be like all the other women who'd ever thrown themselves at him. Feisty and argumentative? Made him desire her more than any other woman.

So why am I letting her think she controls the situation?

Time she understood she didn't.

He helped her from the bed, holding her steady when her knees wobbled.

"They feel like spaghetti," she grumbled. "And don't you dare follow me in. I can wipe my own parts from here on in, thank you." She wouldn't let him into the bathroom, hanging on to the plywood countertop with its stainless-steel bowl sink.

"Try not to fall off the toilet and give yourself a concussion."

"I will do my best," she sassed before shutting the thin door. And locking it.

He refrained from laughing.

As she took care of business, water running and everything, he moved across the space, keeping out of sight of the window until he could stand by the curtain's edge and peek out.

It had been well over twelve hours since

he'd last sighted any of Parker's men in the woods. The hired soldiers spent time and wasted resources—along with lives—hunting for Tomas. The irony was that he hunkered here in the cabin, practically under their noses.

The humans, though, couldn't smell him. They relied on their less-than-perfect senses, which meant they were easy to pick off, at least in the small numbers he'd encountered so far. But Tomas knew his luck couldn't last. They couldn't stay here much longer.

He cast one last glance outside before heading back across the room, the water having shut off in the bathroom. He reached the door a moment after she opened it. Chandra stepped out, looking refreshed, her skin dewy, a cloud of air freshener pouring out around her.

"Say one thing," she growled, her cheeks pink in embarrassment. "This never happens to heroines in the movies."

"Are you comparing our reality to a movie?" he asked, escorting her back to the bedroom.

"You have to admit, it would make for a good one. Brilliant young scientist is kidnapped by nefarious underground medical group but manages to escape with patient zero."

"Hardly zero. I hear they have another like me." Parker had alluded to it once by accident when he thought Tomas unconscious. But Tomas heard it. Heard the reference to gold.

Impossible. All the Golds are dead.

"I am not surprised they do. From what Parker bragged to me, Bittech and the others have been experimenting on so many people." She grouped Tomas into the crowd with all the other lesser species Parker played with.

"So is this the part of the movie where the heroine realizes the hero is male perfection and throws herself at him?" He waggled his brows. He never waggled his brows. He wondered if they were possessed.

She laughed. "You wish."

He did wish. And he would have it, dammit.

Spinning her before she could sit on the bed, he grabbed her, lifted her right off her feet, and kissed her.

Kissed her thoroughly, leaving no part of her mouth untouched.

Kissed her with passion because his blood fired so hot.

Kissed her as if he would never let her go because the simple truth was, while he could claim all he wanted that he did it to prove a point, to show her who was boss, the real reason he kissed her—and couldn't stop kissing her—was because he wanted to. Wanted to taste that mouth again. Wanted to claim it and own it, forever and—

"I found something!"

The distant shout of an intruder tore Tomas out of the moment, and he lifted his head, breaking the kiss.

Danger.

He pulled away and could have roared in frustration at the soft expression on Chandra's face. How dare someone interrupt when her eyes shone so brightly with passion, and her lips were pouted, swollen and inviting?

"What's wrong?" she asked.

"Someone is coming." Several someones. Several dead someones. He'd show them to respect their betters.

A crease marred her brow. "Are you sure? I don't hear anything."

"They're getting close."

"They?" Fear replaced the shine of arousal in her eyes. "Should we run? Hide?"

Emasculating. Cowardly. He shuddered. "You forgot the only real option—fight."

She recoiled. "You can't seriously expect us to fight. We don't have any weapons."

"There is no *we*. Just me. You'll stay here while I take care of this." And by take care of, he meant fertilize the forest with blood. It worked wonders on struggling grass.

"I can't stay here while you go out and fight alone." She sounded incredulous.

"Good point. What if they've surrounded the place and are planning to come in via the back while I'm distracted out front?"

She blinked. "I think I'm going to be sick."

"Try not to hit me if you do."

She glared. "This isn't funny.

"Only because you're still feeling unwell. I should have realized with your fragile human constitution that you weren't ready yet for strenuous activity."

"This has nothing to do with readiness, but the fact that people are coming after us. We need a plan."

She needed to calm down. He reached out to stroke her lower lip with his thumb. "I have a plan. Take care of them."

"How? You're just one man. Without a gun. Or did you find a weapon?" Said with a hopeful lilt.

He shook his head.

"Then how can you act so nonchalant?"

"It's called confidence, doctor. Come watch it in action. Follow me." He gripped her hand and tugged her toward the bedroom door.

"Follow you? But you're going to fight. What am I supposed to do? I don't even have something to defend myself with."

"All you need to do is look pretty." Priceless things shouldn't have to get dirty.

"You did not seriously just say that. I have a Bachelor of Science degree and one for biotechnology. I am more than just a pretty exterior."

"Why can't you just say thank you for the compliment?"

"Because."

He sighed. "Fine. You want a job, then here's one for you. Watch my rear. If you see someone coming, tap me on the shoulder, and I will take care of it."

"You are not taking this seriously."

In that, he disagreed. He was in complete warrior mode now. Holding her by the hand, he stepped farther into the main room and glanced out the window. He spotted at least three figures moving from the forest edge in a tightening circle around the cottage. This was very serious.

"Are you ignoring me?"

"That would be impossible, doctor, since you never stop talking."

They had made it only halfway across the

room when he heard the order. "Fire."

"Get on the floor." Tomas no sooner gave the command than he tripped Chandra to the ground, taking the brunt of the fall as glass exploded all around them.

Chapter Ten

The impact against the floor stole Chandra's breath. The thing was, she couldn't even be mad about the violent takedown or the male body squishing her. Someone had attacked the cabin!

The bullets themselves didn't make much noise as they whistled past, the sharp cracks of the guns occurring outside. As the missiles slammed into the wood paneling, it showered everything with splinters. Not that any hit her. Tomas provided a rather encompassing shield.

The protective gesture, though, did little to warm the icy chill in her veins. They were under attack.

"Stay low," he warned before rolling off her.

She almost rolled her eyes because, really, what idiot would stand with people shooting?

Tomas crab-walked his way to the window and not the door, which now sported several holes. The finger-sized peepholes letting in daylight had her swallowing hard. She already had a scar from the first time she'd run into Parker's employees. She didn't need another.

More bullets peppered the exterior of the house, while still others whistled through the broken window, looking for fleshy targets. Tomas might have said to stay still; however, she felt exposed out in the middle of the floor.

Chandra slid on her belly, trying not to imagine the broken glass and splinters embedding themselves with sharp glee into her skin. She took cover behind the couch, remaining low, the puffs of stuffing a reminder that the sofa would not protect.

A flurry of gunshots had her closing her eyes and praying.

Devi, keep me safe. And keep Tomas safe. Much as she didn't want to die, she didn't want to see him harmed either.

"Holy shit, he's coming." Screamed by a man's voice, followed by lots of jumbled yelling interspersed with the retorts of weapons. So much gunfire.

Chandra clasped her hands over her ears and kept her eyes cinched tight.

Please. Please. Please.

The gunfire stopped for a moment, and she realized she was still alive. She didn't leak from any new holes. Good sign, but what of Tomas?

She had to know.

Taking a deep breath, she peeked around the corner of the couch. She noted the floor covered in debris. Big, black, mud-crusted boots sitting by the closed door. A pile of clothes under the window.

Blink. *I recognize that T-shirt.* Last she'd seen it, a certain large man had worn it.

He stripped to change his shape. She shouldn't have been surprised. He'd never hidden that he wasn't human.

But what is he? He'd alluded, but she'd yet to truly figure it out.

"Argh." The scream abruptly halted, and there was a pause, a tense silence before more gunfire erupted.

Then another scream, long and drawn-out, the height of terror and pain.

She clapped her hands over her ears once more, but she couldn't entirely muffle the sound of more gunfire. In the gaps between the shooting, she also discerned yelling, none of it close by.

It got quiet. So quiet. She pulled her hands from her ears.

Still silent.

She held her breath, but it didn't change the stillness in the air. On hands and knees, watching for glass, she scooted to the window, staying below the level of the sill.

Still no noise. She counted to ten before she dared to peek over the window ledge.

And saw nothing.

The cabin sat in a small clearing bereft of anything but knee-high weeds and wildflowers. It looked so pretty and benign until someone off to the left started begging, "No, don't. Please. Aaah!"

Silence fell once again.

Crunch. Crackle. The sounds of something bulldozing through the underbrush had her ducking down low, but not so low that she missed seeing what emerged from the woods.

She froze for a moment before slowly standing, staring the entire time. How could she not stare? A monster had just emerged from the woods!

Chandra beheld the beast and gulped. Much taller than a man, more around the size of an elephant, with scales an iridescent black and eyes shooting emerald fire.

Dear Devi, he is huge and ferocious. Frightening, too, since she had no trouble imagining the deadly power in that jaw and those claws. Yet, that fear eased something inside her, and she found herself thrilled at finally confirming the existence of a myth in the flesh. His flesh. This monster, this beautiful, majestic beast was Tomas, and Tomas was... "A bloody dragon."

Chapter Eleven

Why did Chandra sound so shocked? Despite her claim that Parker had never told her, he'd alluded to it enough times. Surely, she'd heard some of the news. Even he, during his incarceration, had heard Parker gloating about how the dragons weren't so hidden anymore.

In her defense, media outlets kept debunking the reports that dragons were real. Footage was investigated and supposedly discredited—also known as the Septs covering up their existence.

However, now that she knew the truth, had seen him in the flesh, it peeved Tomas that Chandra chose to act shocked instead of awed by his magnificence. And then she had the nerve to complain.

"Why couldn't you just tell me? Why did you keep playing that stupid guessing game?"

You really didn't know, did you? Since he didn't have a mouth that could handle human speech, he had to think the words to her—and no, he preferred not to analyze how that was possible. Humans and dragons weren't supposed to mix, and most definitely not communicate in this most rare and secret of ways.

"No, he did not tell me." Said with obvious disgruntlement.

How interesting that Parker had kept the secret to himself. If that were the case, then had she perhaps told the truth about other things? Could she be trusted?

Didn't matter either way. He'd decided to claim her.

Since when?

Since I first smelled her.

She approached him, studying him with her head tilted at an inquisitive angle. "This is amazing. Incredible. A real, live dragon."

Disgruntlement grew in him as he noticed that her excitement was curious in nature.

"So this is why Parker wanted you. He wanted your dragon genes. What do you think he did with them?"

Nothing. Because he'd never gotten the samples he wanted from Tomas because Tomas never shifted. *I think.*

A sound in the forest had her turning her head sharply.

It's only a squirrel. Not even a proper-sized snack.

She relaxed. "I am going to assume you took care of all those attackers."

As if there was any doubt.

"Since we're safe for the moment, think you can point me in the direction of civilization? I'm sure you want to leave and go do dragon stuff."

Yes, he did want to leave. What he didn't understand was why she insisted on shrieking when he took her with him.

It took no effort at all to clasp her in his dragon-sized paws. Surely, she didn't think he'd fall out of the tree he climbed—because contrary to belief, he couldn't just take flight in the middle of the forest. Branches cracked, and the trunk began a serious list to the side, but he cleared the boughs enough to throw himself into the air to the sounds of her shrieks.

Good thing he'd taken care of those soldiers, since she'd just pinpointed their location. A few powerful pushes of his wings kept them aloft rather than crashing back into the forest. But did she show any appreciation?

"Put me down before you drop me."

Did she seriously think him so clumsy? Didn't she understand he wouldn't let her come to harm? Tomas protected the things he claimed. Thing was, he couldn't exactly tell her that. Humans didn't understand a dragon's connection to his hoard.

I could try and explain. Explain that she won't come to harm and to trust in the connection we have.

A connection he really should ignore.

The same way I ignored her lips?

That was a mistake caused by captivity and simple, carnal need. Once he returned to his aerie and his life, he'd solve that coital itch.

With her. I shall keep her forever.

The thought caught him, and he faltered mid-stroke. Surely, he wasn't thinking of something permanent with Chandra. In that direction led the big E—emotional entanglement. Which could then turn into heartache and depression. He wasn't keen on collecting those emotions again.

Before that could happen, he'd have to sever things. He'd play with her for a time and, when he became bored, move on.

If that was the plan, then why did he bring her via air current and wing to his hidden home? He didn't allow anyone into his most secret of places. But he currently intended for her to see it. A human.

Because she'sss mine.

He wasn't in the mood to argue with himself. Especially since he could justify breaking his usual rule because she would be in danger if taken anywhere else. By now, Parker and his forces would realize Tomas held her captive.

Prisssoner of your love… His dragon self practically snorted.

Be quiet. He did not love her.

But he did like her. A little too much.

I'd like her even better with fewer clothes.

He'd been such a gentleman when she was ill. Keeping her covered with a sheet as he bathed her skin, not even allowing himself to look as he ran a damp cloth over her to wipe the sweat.

It was easy to ignore her attributes when she lay there dying. Now, she wiggled in his grip and threatened to curse his manhood.

"I swear, if you don't put me down…"

You'll do what?

She mentioned something truly vile. So he dropped her.

He watched her as she plunged, her eyes widening, arms and legs spreading wide.

Given how dense a human body was, she fell rather fast from the height he'd brought them—

high enough to glide through the misty clouds and hide himself. He didn't worry about radar giving away his position. His scales took care of all signals that might betray him.

Tomas waited until he was sure Chandra had learned her lesson and plunged. He dove past her and rolled under her, letting her hit his belly, the softest part of him. He caught her before she could roll off, his wings extended in a glide.

She lay on his dragon chest for a moment before saying, "You are such a jerk."

A real jerk would have let her play with gravity to the end.

What did Tomas have to do to get her thanks? At least he'd quelled her complaining. She no longer asked him to put her down. He kind of missed her lively threats.

It took the rest of the daylight hours and several of the night ones for him reach the mountain he wanted. He'd long ago had to tuck Chandra close to his chest as he flew, doing his best to block the wind from her shivering body. She wasn't dressed for flight.

He coasted onto the top of a thin spire, no more than a dozen feet across and fluting downwards, the sides jagged as parts of it sloughed off each year.

Only someone who could fly could reach it, and then, they'd have to contend with the security system he'd put in place.

Setting Chandra down, Tomas moved away from her, not far given the lack of room on the narrow plateau. With only a little force of will, he drew his dragon back inside, compressed all his lovely lightness into a compact human form. It felt so tight and constraining. It was also quite chilly, given he returned to his man shape quite naked.

Overjoyed by his masculine presence, Chandra launched herself at him. Fists flew as she pounded on his chest. He stood still while she pummeled, massaging his muscles. It truly did relax, and he fought not to yawn. When she slowed, Tomas looked down and asked her, quite nicely he thought, "Ready to do my back?"

"Jerk." She stomped his foot, eliciting a pained wince.

"For a woman who claimed she couldn't do violence, you do quite well against me."

"What can I say? You bring out the best in me."

"I'd like to put my best into you." Said with a wide smile.

"We are not having sex."

"Not here. Or now. Someone needs to bathe." He wrinkled his nose.

Her jaw dropped, and she looked quite aghast. "Did you just say I smell?"

"You do. But fear not. I have bathing facilities in the aerie that will rectify that problem."

She planted her hands on her hips and looked around. "Really? Because I don't see anything remotely resembling a shower."

"Because it is inside. Really, doctor, I'm beginning to wonder if your educational diplomas were from real institutions." Moving past her, he found a cluster of rocks that appeared a jumbled mess. Placing his hand and most of his forearm into the hole, he pressed it against a palm reader that would recognize only him. Anyone else would lose their arm. Cousin Jorje had had a hard time explaining how he'd happened to misplace his limb at their last family gathering.

Only the slightest grinding of mechanical parts filled the air, but Tomas knew the entrance opened simply by Chandra's exclaimed, "You have a hidden lair."

Lair? He liked the sound of that.

Tomas turned and offered his hand. "You might want to hold on to me. It's a little drop from the top."

She craned to peek over the lip of the trapdoor. Her eyes widened as she backed away. "Little drop? I can barely see the bottom."

"If you did, then you'd note it is Italian polished marble, recovered from a chapel that was destroyed decades ago in a minor quake. Beautifully crafted stuff."

"Very hard stuff, too, as in Chandra"—she pointed to herself—"would go splat." She slapped her hands together.

"It's a great way to tenderize meat."

The comment served only to widen her eyes to the point that he feared they'd fall out.

"Do you really think I brought you here to eat you?" He smiled. "You're right. I did."

He thought the wink would make it clear what kind of eating he meant, but instead, she backed away from him, her feet sliding on the wind-polished surface, precariously close to the edge.

Enough of the games. The longer they stood out here, the more chances his enemy had to spot him.

Lunging, he grabbed the doctor around the waist before she could topple. He immediately curved and dove toward the hole in the spire.

She screamed and clung to him.

He laughed.

Welcome to the aerie. The home of the most exclusive collection in all the Septs.

Having done this leap many times before, he knew what to expect, but Chandra clung tight to him the entire way down, whispering, "Save me, Devi, from his madness."

On the contrary, the Indian goddess Devi should play for my side since I have untold wealth to please. And he would pay dearly for the privilege of having Chandra. That became clearer and clearer the more time he spent with her.

Despite the steep drop, the spells in this place were attuned to him, and he alit with hardly a bump. Only when he cleared his throat and said, "We've arrived," did Chandra peer from his shoulder.

"We're not dead."

"As if there was any doubt." He set Chandra down, and she stepped away from him, more awed by what she saw than the fact that Tomas remained denuded and out of the cold wind, quickly recovering his stature.

She spun around and craned to look. "What is this place? It's incredible."

I am incredible. But his treasure house was pretty awesome, too. "This is my home when I'm not working at the university or on a dig."

"Home?" She whirled to look at him. "But it's in a mountain."

"Indeed. I happened to find it when exploring as a teen. I don't know who initially carved it." He knew wizards often built hidden hideaways, but this seemed elaborate and the scale of it vast.

The room they'd dropped into started out narrow and widened, just as the stone spire thickened until it opened into a large, very large, chamber lit by strategic fissures chiseled into the rock and lined with crystals. It prevented water and the elements from entering but kept the air fresh, and during the daytime, the room sparkled as brightly as the outside.

"What is all this stuff?" She wandered away from him and began to trail a finger over the pedestals that dotted the outer perimeter of the room.

"My hoard." On display were the things that held value—to Tomas. A priceless vase alongside a commendation from a colleague on an achievement in the archeological world. A gold-plated statue from the Mesopotamia era sat adjacent to a giant, pinkish-gray wad.

She pointed. "What is that?"

"The most gum I ever managed to stuff into my mouth at once."

"And you kept it?" She rounded on him with her mouth agape.

"Personal achievements are priceless."

She shook her head. "You're a very strange man, Tomas."

"But a very normal dragon."

"If you say so. You're the first one I've officially met. Were you always a dragon?"

His turn to gape at her. "What an inane question. I was always a dragon. One does not simply become a dragon." Never mind the rumors he'd heard of a Silvergrace girl marrying such a fellow.

"Well, now that I know you're real, I have to wonder because I could have sworn I saw some kind of gossip claiming otherwise. Didn't a movie star give birth to a litter of lizards?"

"No, she did not. You shouldn't listen to rumors."

"Usually, I don't because I prefer factual science, but sometimes, within the rumor is a hint of truth."

"Here's the truth—dragons cannot be made."

"Some say Brandon, Parker's nephew, got turned into one."

He waved a hand. "And other media reports debunked it as a hoax. The boy was simply looking to get attention and funding for his uncle's company by claiming something impossible." Or so the Septs wanted to believe. Tomas had to wonder, given Brandon, a gator shifter from the wrong side of a whole bunch of tracks, married a precious Silvergrace daughter. Either the girl was living in disgrace, or there was something more at play.

"If dragons aren't made, then why did Parker keep you prisoner? What use were you to him?"

"I told you before. I wasn't a prisoner. I was there investigating."

"You were kept in chains and drugged."

"You make it sound worse than it was. My

every need, including that of sleep, was taken care of." He amended that statement. "Almost every need. The shower is that way." He pointed.

She didn't scurry.

He would really prefer she bathed first.

Rather than strip and run for cleanliness, she crossed her arms. "Are you suggesting I bathe so you can have sex with me?"

"I was suggesting no such thing." He couldn't help but sound affronted. "I was demanding it. Bathe. Now. I won't have your fouled body in my bed."

"Your bed won't be getting any of my body because I am not having sex with you."

The idea perplexed. "Why not? I've saved you numerous times. You are attracted to me. Is it because I've not offered you recompense? Would a matching diamond jewelry set do? Or do you prefer another stone?"

Wrong question. Her eyes narrowed. "I will not be bought or coerced."

"Then what will it take? Ask for it. I have plenty to give. Except for that." He pointed to his third-grade Thanksgiving project that involved a meticulously traced and cut-out version of his hand then decorated into a turkey. He was quite proud of that piece of art, especially since his grandmother deemed it the most perfect fowl she'd ever seen.

"How about common decency? Respect. Maybe accepting the fact that I'm not interested in a physical relationship."

"You'll change your mind." She had to because, otherwise, his balls would shrivel and fall off, little blue marbles that would require a pedestal with a handy box of tissues so he could cry at the loss of his manhood.

Did she really think she could resist him?

She certainly paid him no mind, walking past him with a snarky, "I am going to shower, but not because you ordered it, and not because we're having sex, but because I do stink. Of dragon."

Of all the insults!

She's so utterly perfect.

One moment, feminine and in needing of his protection; the next, bringing him low with mere words and sass.

A part of him thought he should go after her and join her in the shower—fed by a brilliant cistern system that captured rain and dew.

But he'd already abased himself enough for this woman. Let her miss him and come crawling back to bask in his greatness.

His un-admired, naked greatness.

He scowled down at his body. He'd lost weight during his tenure at the secret lab. Perhaps that was why she found him unappealing.

As she bathed, he also took a shower, using a kitchen sink hose that proved invigorating and sluiced down a drain in the floor. It made cleaning up blood so much easier.

He had time to grab a robe and garb himself, make a sandwich—the frozen ingredients only showing a few signs of frost burn—before she reappeared.

She also wore a robe and a towel on her head. Her feet were bare, the toes long and unpainted. Her ankles trim, and her calves—

"You can stop that right now." She tucked

the robe tighter.

"I see the bathing did not improve your mood. Sandwich?" He held out the other half of his third sandwich, the chicken breast thick, the bacon crunchy, the mayo giving it extra flavor to complement the cheese. It just missed lettuce and tomato for utter perfection.

"You really do live here, don't you?" she noted, taking the sandwich from his hand. "Doesn't that make it hard to commute to work?"

"I don't stay here when teaching. I have an apartment close to campus for that."

"Then why have this place? Couldn't you just get yourself a house and have all your stuff with you full-time?"

"Expose my collection to possible thieves?" He almost recoiled. "Do you know nothing at all of dragons?"

"No. Thought to be fake, remember?"

How true. And yet, now that she knew of him, there was surely no harm in giving her a brief lesson.

"To start, dragons are the top of the chain."

"What chain?"

"*The* chain. The one that starts with dragons then the fey. Followed by the merpeople, although the mountain folk, those you call dwarves, are disputing that hierarchy."

"Where do humans fit on the list?" she asked.

"A bit farther down. Under the dolphins, but above household pets." At her glare, he added. "There is a petition to have them moved."

"I see. Do you have a pen and paper?" she

asked.

"You wish to take notes. How remiss of me." He commended her wanting to learn about him. Perhaps then she would better understand the futility of arguing with him.

A desk—the same one he'd done his homework on growing up and kept as a cherished possession—held a spot of honor in the room and provided the tools he needed. Chandra, who'd seated herself in the meantime on a huge sectional sofa—brought in piece by piece as if he were nothing more than a delivery boy—propped the notebook on her lap and wrote.

Dragon Facts.

1. Arrogant

2. Bossy

He pointed at it. "Don't forget narcissistic and covetous, as well as protective of our territory."

She paused with the pen against her lips. "Are you not bothered at all by the fact that you're quite immodest?"

"Modesty is for those who lack greatness."

She shook her head and wrote a few more notes. *Born, not made. Approximate size, five meters tall.*

"Weight?"

His lips quirked as he said, "A dragon never tells."

"Is it hard to stay in your dragon shape?"

"Being in my natural state is a form of euphoria. It is when I am in this shape that I feel compressed and uncomfortable."

"Does it hurt when you change?"

"Pain is but a fleeting thing."

"I don't like pain."

"I'll protect you from it." The promise hung heavily in the air between them.

"So, how many dragons are there in the world?"

"I don't keep count, although I am sure the Septs have a vague idea of their numbers."

"What are Septs?"

"Think of them as a form of governance. Much like how the royals used to rule. Each Sept is made up of numerous families and is led by the matriarch of the strongest one."

"Women are your bosses?"

"The strongest rule the Septs. It just so happens that, given that the birth rate of males can be rather low, females often manage to commandeer the position." It didn't help that most males had lost their alpha gene over the centuries and proved quite content to let the women rule. Except for Tomas. Tomas still had his balls and didn't plan to give them to any woman.

Okay, maybe one woman could play with them...but that wouldn't make him less of a man.

"So what Sept do you belong to?"

"Alas, I am one of the rare dragons that have no Sept to call my own. When I ascended, it was discovered I have no color."

"What do you mean no color? You're like a sparkling ebony."

"You think I sparkle?" The adjective pleased because it meant she noticed.

"The Septs are divided into colors? I thought you said it was comprised of families."

"It is, but those families are also predominantly one hue. Even when bloodlines are mixed, one color emerges strongest."

"And you—"

"Am what they call a Wilder. I am all colors and none. I can belong anywhere."

"But you chose…"

"None." Because all the families saw in him was a stud, a male to make babies for the Sept.

Tomas wasn't sure about ever having children because then he might get attached to them. What if they didn't like him or tried to touch his things?

Best not attempt it.

"So you're like a lone wolf."

He shuddered. "Do not compare me to mangy curs."

The pen tapped against her lips. He knew of something that wanted to trade places.

"You don't like shifters, do you? And yet, aren't you in the same family?"

His brows rose. "Don't let my grandmother hear you say that." She'd made people disappear for less.

She leaned forward, determined to argue further. "But you both change from human to animal shapes."

"They're animals. We are dragons. We eat animals."

She scribbled on her pad: *carnivore*.

"With a sweet tooth. Especially for caramel."

She added that and *outrageous flirt*.

"Do you have brothers and sisters?"

At the question, his levity vanished. "No."

"Parents?"

"Dead in the same crash." The one he was

spared because he'd begged to spend the night at his grandparents', else he, too, would have been in the deadly accident that took his parents' and younger siblings' lives. His kind might heal exceptionally well, but the fiery inferno that remained after the tractor-trailer had slammed into his parents' Escalade left nothing but bones and ash.

"I'm sorry."

"Why? You didn't know them, and I managed quite fine despite it." His grandparents had taken him in and done their best.

So why did he leave them and now rarely talk to them?

Because of the fear I'll lose them, too. With distance, he couldn't feel anything if something happened.

"How do you procreate? Are dragons like lizards where the female lays an egg, and the male fertilizes it?"

"That would take most of the fun out of it." Although, in ages past, according to history, when dragons lived in their true form on a daily basis, that was exactly how the females chose to reproduce. And he meant females. The males didn't care so long as they had young to carry on their great name.

"Can you only impregnate your kind?"

"It is recommended, given couplings between humans and dragons result in wyverns."

"Isn't that another name for a dragon?"

Again, he couldn't help a snort of disdain. "No. Wyverns are much less superior, un-ascended versions. They are also sterile and male only. Their worst attribute is that they are scentless, which is quite annoying given how sneaky they are."

"What's un-ascended supposed to mean?"

"Can we not save the biology lessons for another day? Or, even better, if you're so interested in form, then you may study mine."

"I've seen yours. Got any other examples I can examine instead?"

The mere suggestion of her looking upon another sent him into a bit of a jealous rage. Before he could think, or she could breathe, he sat beside her on the couch. Close. So close he could smell she'd used his shampoo on her hair. His soap on her body.

His hand cupped the back of her head, threading his fingers through her thick hair, the damp tendrils clinging to him as he angled her head back.

"What are you doing?" The words emerged on a soft whisper.

"What's it look like I'm doing, doctor? Surely a bright woman like you can figure it out."

"I told you no more kissing." Said with eyes at half-mast, lips parted, and a heartbeat that sped up.

"Then stop me."

He slanted his mouth over hers, pressing his lips firmly while waiting for her to protest. Would she struggle to put a stop to the kiss? Would she bite?

Tomas wouldn't force her—but he would do his best to seduce.

In between nibbles, she still managed to speak. "We really shouldn't do this."

"Yes, we should."

And he would. She'd tempted him long enough. He dragged her onto his lap, her spot beside him too far. She didn't protest, instead turning on his lap that she might cup his face in her hands. She kissed him just as hungrily. Seeming needy.

He also needed this.

Needed her.

Earlier, he'd found excuses to touch her. No more. He wanted Chandra. Wanted her sweetness and softness, wanted a taste of her.

For just a moment, he broke the embrace, his breathing not as smooth as he'd like, his erection firm against her ass. "Still want to tell me to stop?"

For a moment, her eyes opened, heavy with desire. Her lips curved. "Are you telling me you can?"

"No. I need you." He couldn't believe he admitted it out loud and immediately sought to cover his gaffe by covering her mouth with his. His arms crushed her tightly as their lips meshed in a torrid kiss that left her panting.

But kissing wasn't enough. He slid his lips away from her mouth, down the column of her throat, stopping at the flutter of her pulse. He kissed that beating reminder of life, and her breathing hitched.

"You don't bite, do you?" she asked, her tone part trepidation, part excitement.

"I make no promises."

"Oh." Not no. Not don't. Oh. A soft exhalation as she dipped her head back and exposed more of that throat to him.

Such trust.

So tempting.

His hands cradled her upper body as he bent her back, allowing his lips to move past her neck to her collarbone, nudging the fabric of her robe open that he might kiss the swell of her breast.

Her fingers clutched at his shoulders, and she moaned as he caught the tip of a nipple with his lips. He tugged it, pulling it taut, and heard her sob a breath of air.

He sucked it, and she cried out. She shifted on him, squirming, the opening to her robe widening, releasing the scent of her arousal.

She wants me.

He could smell the honey. He wanted the honey.

He laid her back on the couch and covered her, capturing her lips once again as he one-handedly undid the knot keeping her hidden from him. He spread the robe open before resuming his exploration, his mouth capturing and toying with each of her breasts before giving in to the temptation and rubbing past the soft skin of her belly.

She wore no underpants, and she didn't shave. A woman au naturel. How decadent. He rubbed his face over her mound, and she gasped.

"You smell good," words practically growled against her skin. And it must have frightened her, for she tried to press her thighs together.

"Open for me," he said, blowing at the crease of her thighs. "I want to taste you."

"I—I…" She tried to speak, failed, and her thighs relaxed, spread enough that he could fan his warm breath over her nether lips. The wet tip of his tongue traced her outer shell, a slow and languorous touch that drew a moan from her.

The sound emboldened him to take a proper taste. He licked her, tasting the sweet honey just for him.

"Oh." Again, he licked her, pressing his tongue between her lips, thrusting it deep.

Chandra heaved on the couch, her fingers clutching at the cushions as he aroused her.

He moved from the couch to the floor and angled her so that her legs hung over his shoulders. Her moist flesh beckoned, and she moaned as he returned to licking the sweet spot between her thighs. He lapped and teased her slit before circling his tongue around her clit. With his lips alone, he held and sucked on her sensitive nub. She bucked and cried out. All of her quivered.

Tomas rested a hand on her stomach and held her still, pinned her that he might continue to suckle at her clit. Deep moans and soft cries were the music he licked to. He knew she approached the peak of pleasure as her back arched, her whole body tense.

He stopped for a moment and stared. Stared at the smooth expanse of skin exposed to him, her breasts each a perky handful jutting proudly with erect tips. Her belly flat. Such perfection.

Her eyes opened, and her lips parted.

He wished he could have that image, this moment in time, frozen forever.

But he was too impatient to fetch a camera. Instead, he shed his robe, and this time when he stripped, exposing his lean, hard body, he saw the admiration in her gaze.

He thrust his shoulders back as she reached out and stroked her hand down his chest. She stopped at his navel.

"You can touch," he told her.

A red hue flooded her cheeks, and she averted her gaze.

Her shyness hinted at inexperience. He'd thought he couldn't get any harder. He was wrong.

His erect cock, which tilted upwards at the tip, extended proudly from his loins and throbbed with need.

Need her.

Denuded, and with her still acting shyly, Tomas returned to his licking and soon had her panting, her body undulating.

He wanted her to come for him, to come against his lips and cry out with pleasure. He growled against her sex before moving up until his body covered hers, the skin-to-skin contact scorching. His hard cock was trapped between their bodies and pressed against the seam of her thighs. He latched his lips onto hers, and he opened her mouth with the insistent probe of his tongue.

The hard pebbles of her nipples dug into his chest, and Tomas suddenly couldn't resist their call. He broke their embrace that he might bend and take one into his mouth. As his tongue swirled around the tip, Chandra moaned and clutched at his head. Her hips bucked under him, and her whole body trembled as she pressed closer.

Her desire, his desire, hung heavy in the air. Their pleasure was at a peak, and Tomas couldn't help but utter a sound of satisfaction.

Eyelids, heavy with desire, lifted, and she looked at him. Truly looked at him, and her eyes widened.

"Your eyes are glowing."

"You do this to me," he admitted. "You unleash the beast in me."

Her breathing hitched.

"Don't be afraid," he murmured against her mouth. "Never afraid."

He dipped his head for a kiss, a masterful embrace that claimed her mouth as his. She returned it, her passion just as fierce.

He dipped a hand between their bodies and found her sex. He dipped his finger in the honey, wetting it before circling it on her clit.

She cried into his mouth, and her fingers dug into his shoulders as he played with her.

"Come for me," he whispered against her lips. Come, and then as her channel still shuddered from her first climax, he would slide into her and take her over the edge with a second orgasm.

She undulated under him. Her breathing so ragged, her moans more sobs of pleasure as she reached her peak.

He pinched her nub, pinched it as he kissed her, and her body arched. Held. Her breathing stopped.

"Tomas." She exhaled, one word. One word only.

His name.

"Tomas."

Mine.

And yet before he could fully claim her, before he could stamp her with his body, someone just had to interrupt.

Chapter Twelve

"Don't move," he growled as parts of her still throbbed. Chandra ached with a satisfaction she'd never managed on her own. And forget her first husband. She'd known more than he did about how to pleasure herself.

Not so with Tomas. He didn't need help. Tomas knew exactly where to touch her. Where to kiss her. How to make her body sing.

And make me forget every single moral I possess.

The blissful waves slowly subsided, and she waited for the shame to hit. Maybe a heaping of guilt? After all, she'd been raised to think of her body as a precious temple. Not just anyone could be allowed to worship. Yet, despite all her promises to herself, all the claims she made, she couldn't resist when Tomas touched her. She didn't want to resist.

This was the missing component she'd always heard about when it came to sex. This was passion.

"Where are you going?" Because, for some reason, despite the erection jutting, Tomas moved away from her. Were they done?

As if reading her mind, he replied, "That is just the beginning, doctor."

"What do you mean?" Surely, he couldn't do anything more to her? Or could he? Parts of her tingled, anticipation making her skin flush as she wondered what might happen next.

What happened was something rang. Loudly. Insistently. And he reacted as if someone had shot him.

He stood, naked and proud, with his hands on his hips. "Computer, who is calling?"

A melodious voice replied. "It is actually a text message from the Mauve Sept, advising you to watch the news."

"Now?"

As Tomas grumbled about cock-blocking family members who screwed with him even from miles away, Chandra snuck off to the washroom to rinse herself off and regain her composure. The shame of what she'd done hadn't hit, but incredulity did.

I let that man touch me. Touch me intimately.

More shocking, she wanted him to touch her again without any kind of promise or even a working relationship. They were pretty much captor and captive. She should be fighting him, not melting in his arms.

She heard him bellow, "Are they bloody mad?"

What had him so angry? She dried her face and hands before stepping out.

Tomas stomped back and forth in his living area, his sizable frame dwarfed by the enormous television screen that now projected images on the far wall.

"What's wrong?" she asked.

A glower pulled his brows together. "Parker and the Crimson Sept, those red, power-hungry bastards, have gone too far. There will be no hiding our presence now. No more coming up with brilliant excuses."

"What's happened?" She peeked around him, but the news on-screen was muted, and the speaking newscasters, while animated, gave nothing away.

"What's happened is, according to CNN, the Reds have held a conference, one recorded by too many to refute, and left absolutely no doubt that dragons exist."

"What's wrong with that? I mean, I get you'd prefer they didn't know, but unlike werewolves, most people like dragons. They're cool."

"Exactly. People love us. As trophies. Do you not read history at all, doctor?"

"Yes, but dragons aren't a part of human history."

He arched a brow. "Aren't they? Don't you know of any fables that tell of the killing of dragons? Usually as part of a quest. Or because someone needed an ingredient."

"Are you talking about fairy tales where knights kill the rampaging dragon to save a princess?"

"There were never any princesses to save. We tend to avoid them because of their histrionics. And they're tough to chew. We prefer soft and plump matrons. Bakers are quite tasty, too, especially when rolled in icing sugar."

She couldn't help but roll her eyes. "And

with a conversation like that, one has to wonder how you've managed to stay hidden so long."

"Because humans don't want to believe." He shrugged as he turned away. He pointed to the newscaster. "Even now. That woman on screen, despite the evidence being shoved in her face, is still convinced everything is a gimmick. A sham. And mostly, they're right. It worked quite to our advantage. Until now. Damned Reds. What are they thinking?"

"So what does this mean for you?" Was he worried he would now be hunted?

He turned his gaze on her. "It means nothing. Just because the Reds have come out, along with the Blues, doesn't mean I plan to. Humanity is too quick to grab a sword when it comes to my kind."

"Ignoring reality. There's a plan."

"The Reds are the ones imposing this mess. Let them deal with the fallout. I am perfectly fine continuing my existence in the shadows."

"Well, I'm not hiding away. Now that Parker has some dragons, surely we're safe now."

"I wouldn't necessarily count on that."

"And exactly what is that supposed to mean? What are you planning now?"

"Now…" His mood turned lightning quick. "Now, we finish what we began."

Except what they'd begun couldn't happen. As he stalked toward her, his eyes dark with intent, she held up a hand. "While I truly enjoyed what we did"—huge blush—"it can't happen again."

"Why ever not?"

"Because I'm not the type of girl who does

this kind of thing."

"But I am the type of man who does. So that counteracts your complaint."

By the sweet goddess, the man was stubborn. She stood and confronted him. "You cannot keep bullying me into doing what you want."

"Then I will kiss you into compliance. Again."

She danced out of his reach and shook her head. "No, you won't. I'm sorry, but I need you to take me home."

"Your home is not safe."

"I'll take that chance." Because staying here with him wasn't safe either.

"You're being stubborn."

"So are you."

His expression turned stony. "You won't survive a moment out there without me."

"I used to survive just fine before I met you. You're not the first man in my life who thought I couldn't live without him."

His nostrils flared. "Very well. You wish to leave, then the only way out is through there." He pointed upward. "Good luck growing some wings."

"Don't be a jerk. Obviously, you'll have to help me get out of here."

"What if I refuse?"

She crossed her arms. "I won't be a prisoner."

"I don't see as you have much of a choice."

"I hate you."

"Medical science has proven that the pheromones related to hatred are almost identical to that of lust. So what you're really saying is you're lusting after me."

His logic almost made her laugh, and knowing she softened meant she glared.

The unrepentant smirk didn't move. It was like arguing with a rock. An immovable, sexy rock.

But still, a rock.

"You can't bully me into sleeping with you."

"But I can seduce."

"I'd like to see you try." Really, she would, and mostly because she feared he was right, and she would enjoy it too much.

Bells began to chime, and he rolled his eyes. "Now what? Why is it every time I try to have a conversation—"

"Argument"

"—with you, we are interrupted."

"Is someone attacking?" She'd had quite enough of people trying to harm her, thank you very much.

"It's worse." Tomas eyed a screen and frowned. "My family has chosen to visit."

"Why is that bad?"

"For one thing, it's not done without invitation. And secondly…my grandmother isn't crazy about humans."

"What does that mean?"

"You might want to stick close to me."

Not exactly the most reassuring advice. Chandra, though, refused to cower behind him. Instead, she lifted her chin and tucked the robe tighter.

The bells chimed again. More insistently.

"Aren't you going to answer?"

"Don't say I didn't warn you. And try not to show any fear. She'll use it against you."

"Who will?"

"The matriarch of the Mauve Sept. My grandmother."

Chapter Thirteen

Yes, his damned grandmother.

Of all the ill timing. Ignoring her tempted, but he knew better than to deny her presence.

Grandmother never spared the rod—on man or child. Respect for the matriarch was always maintained.

"Computer, allow sky access to our guest."

"Please verify the command." Because Tomas had never issued the command before.

"Yeah, it's me commanding." Stupid security features. Tomas slapped his palm onto the access panel screen embedded in the breakfast bar countertop. High overhead, the rooftop egress slid open, and a moment later, in swooped a dragon. A rather majestic dragon in light purple tones with hints of gray. Grandmother was getting on in her years.

She also never came to visit. As she grew older, she preferred to remain close to home, near her hoard. Grandmother had quite the collection. She collected the standard riches—gold, jewelry, paintings—but she also had a strange obsession with collectible figurines. She had hundreds of them. All in perfect condition. Their porcelain painted eyes always watching.

As a young boy, Tomas was convinced they were moving. He blamed them for some incidences in the house he'd been raised in. The spilled plant, and the broken-off leg of a dancing gentleman beside it meant Tomas lost dessert privileges for a week.

The shepherd girl that disappeared with the soldier, never to be seen again? Tomas got blamed for that, too, even though he was sure they'd eloped. Who else would be sending postcards from around the world claiming, "Having fun. Wish you were here."

But at least grandmother's hoard obsession could be smashed with a hammer if needed. Grandfather's involved dark arcana books from a time when there were wizards and sorceresses. None had been seen now in centuries, their births rare to start with, and once the dragons chose to eliminate them for aligning with humans in the war, they went extinct.

Dark magic should be destroyed, but instead, Grandfather held it all in one well-hidden bunker.

Tomas had no idea where it was, but remembered seeing it as a child, his grandfather blindfolding him and putting a headset on that muffled all outside sound.

But he didn't need to see to feel the itch of power when his grandfather brought him into the place where he kept his hoard.

It made a dragon want to control the world.

Running the world, though, required a lot of paperwork and dealing with people. Tomas resisted the urge to rampage and become supreme ruler. But even over twenty years later, the feeling still crept up on him. Imagine now, if the wrong person were to find the hoard.

What fun they'd have.

Less fun was dealing with Grandmother. He eyed her with suspicion as she alit and transformed, her frame still as tall as ever, her features just as sharp. The massive size of her dragon compressed into that of a woman with a Rubenesque shape.

"She's naked," Chandra squeaked and hid her face.

"Of course she is. We rarely carry around clothes. It's undignified." Dragons did not put as much stock in nudity as humans did. They also didn't transform often, not of late. With the advent of satellites watching and, more recently still, the rise in the use of drones, discovery became more and more likely.

Parker might have aligned with the Reds to announce it, but it was bound to come out eventually. The world was too connected with video everywhere to keep the secret. Because there was no way dragons could completely stop flying. They needed the skies, the wide space, the feeling of lightness that came with transformation.

Speaking of drones, one emerged from a cubby in the wall, the computer having been programmed to offer robes to guests.

As his grandmother slipped it on, he hit the kitchen to fetch the coffee that would already be brewing. Just because Tomas didn't get visitors didn't mean he'd not planned for them. His computer was programmed to have things work seamlessly. An invisible servant.

"This is unexpected," he said as he placed the carafe of coffee onto the tray with some cups. He didn't add sugar or cream. Only savages ruined perfectly good beans. "You should have called first."

"I did. You didn't call back."

"I would have. Eventually." Not. Tomas had yet to hug his grandmother. He wouldn't because hugging would show he'd missed her. Which meant he cared.

He couldn't care.

Look at her. She was getting old. She maybe only had another fifty to sixty years left.

Better to stay detached now.

"Are you sassing your matriarch, boy?" The arch of the brow. Oh, how he knew that arch. The pressed lips, too.

He almost smiled. *How I've missed it.*

He pressed his lips. *Don't let her know I'm happy to see her.*

"To what do I owe this intrusion?"

"This social call is to ensure your well-being. Word in the Sept was you'd been taken from your last job."

"And you just now came looking?"

"We looked. We just couldn't find you. Do you know how many resources I've expended looking for your ungrateful carcass? And then I find you here. Safe. Unharmed. I should kill you for that."

Tomas heard the undertone—*I'm glad you're not dead because otherwise I would have avenged you.*

The crazy part was, if anybody ever hurt his grandmother, he'd do the same thing.

"I didn't need any help. I just went away for a bit of rest and relaxation."

"You're not going to tell her about Parker kidnapping you and performing experiments?"

Two sets of eyes swung Chandra's way. Did the doctor realize what she'd just done?

His grandmother's voice emerged deceptively quiet. "That dog did what to my grandson?"

Given he knew what that tone meant, Tomas hastened to regain the upper hand. "Nothing you need to worry about. I will take care of Parker."

That served only to completely set his grandmother off. "Did that shifter mongrel dare to kidnap a male of the Mauve Sept? I will shred the flesh from his frame. Boil the marrow in his bones, and drink it. Then I shall—"

"You will do nothing," he shouted, "because it's not your problem."

"Your family will avenge you," Grandmother vowed.

"I have no family." He shook his head and tried, not for the first time, to ignore the hurt in his grandmother's eyes. He'd made his choice to live apart a long time ago, back when everyone thought to use him as some kind of bargaining chip in the marriage market.

He knew it hurt the woman in front of him, the woman who'd raised Tomas after his parents died. His mother, her beloved daughter. Tomas was all his grandparents had left, and yet, it was best they stay apart. If he let himself care, then she, too, might die.

His grandmother's voice boomed, the truth of it ringing loudly enough to shake his mountain. "You are a son of the Amethyst family and will always be welcome in the Mauve Sept. You are not alone, even if you are a stubborn ass."

He wouldn't let the oft-repeated words sneak past his shields. "You only want me so you can have the prestige of marrying me off in order to further the Sept's power base."

"Perhaps that was my goal once. That was before. I've had time to reflect on that decision."

"You have?" He turned a dubious gaze on his grandmother. "Are you going to tell me you don't want me to make babies for the Sept?"

"My desires have never changed. I want to see you continue our line, although I would have preferred you make dragon babies rather than wyvern, but with the Golds returning, you do whatever makes you happy."

A few things struck him as wrong. First, what was this about a Gold returning? And why did she think he was making babies with Chandra? Yes, he lusted after her, but he would most certainly not get her pregnant. There were things to prevent that. "What are you talking about? There are no babies happening. Now, or ever."

"Don't lie to me, boy. Your scent is all over the human, and she is in your aerie. You have obviously chosen."

Chandra interjected. "Oh, I'm not here permanently. Tomas and I were just discussing me leaving."

"You're not leaving." He couldn't stop the words, and almost winced because he knew his grandmother had noticed. Chandra certainly did.

"Oh, yes, I am leaving. You can't keep me prisoner."

"Not according to the four posts of my bed." He didn't have any true manacles, but a tie would work just as well.

"Tomas!" More than one woman's voice shrieked his name.

His grandmother tsked. "Really, Tomas. I understand your need to rebel, but to keep a human against her will?"

"She wants to be here. She just doesn't know it." It sounded lame and stalkerish, even to him. "Chandra is none of your business. *I'm* none of your business. So get to the point of your visit. And then you can explain what you meant when you said a Gold is returning. The Golds are extinct." He should know. He'd been looking for them a good portion of his life. Rumor told that the last Golden hoard contained a treasure beyond compare, one that would change everything.

He'd been looking all his life and had never found it. But he knew from all the research he had done that the Golden Sept dragons did not exist.

"I don't know how it happened, but it seems a Gold has finally returned. And you know what this means."

Of course he did. He'd been raised to hear the gospel of the Gold, the legend and religion that basically promised a war and world domination.

A lot of dragons had flocked to the cultish religion in recent years. With the skies increasingly dangerous to fly, the dragon ranks were restless. They needed something to believe in, something to give them hope that they'd own the skies again.

"So where's this Gold been hiding?"

"We don't know. We still aren't even sure of his location."

He frowned. "Then how do you know he exists?"

"Because we all got the blood."

Tomas rubbed his forehead. "You are going to have to explain because this is getting convoluted." And not what he wanted to be doing, especially since Chandra had long since lost the soft *I came for you* look and appeared entirely serious instead.

"If you perhaps didn't closet yourself, you'd know that all of the Septs received a vial of blood. Beautiful crystal bottles filled to the brim. We had it tested, thinking it was an indication of a hostage situation. Imagine the surprise when the Sept test for color indicated that it was Gold."

"So, on the basis of a vial of blood, you think there's one alive somewhere?" Tomas had his doubts. Did Parker have something to do with this?

"We don't need to see the Gold to know the king returns. The blood speaks for itself. Soon, our kind shall rise and take our rightful place. Our numbers will flourish. It's already started."

"What do you mean?"

"You'll soon see." The ominous words deserved more of an explanation, but his grandmother turned from him and chose to address Chandra. "I was just about to leave. Going back to town. Might I offer you a ride, child?"

The doctor took a step toward his grandmother. "Yes, please."

Yes, please? Chandra didn't mean it. She was a woman, which meant Tomas knew how this game was played. She'd pretend to want to go, expecting him to suddenly throw himself at her and beg her to stay. To declare he cared.

I can't care.

He didn't care.

Let her leave.

Doesn't matter to me.

She turned to look at him, and he could see how she worried her lower lip, stared at him. The flicker of her pulse in her neck ticked faster. He could see she wanted him.

I knew she wouldn't go.

Knew she…wait. What did she do? Why did Chandra raise her arms so that Grandmother might clasp her in her paws and claws? Why did she not protest as they rose to the ceiling, the hidden door sliding open?

Come back.

Don't leave me alone.

Chapter Fourteen

Don't go. Chandra knew the words weren't hers. And yet they were. A part of her had wanted to stay. She'd stared into his eyes, seen the flicker of want in them, seen his smug triumph when she wavered and was about to step toward him.

Instead, she'd walked away. She'd let this massive dragon grab her and fly her out of the aerie, and she shut her eyes against the tears. Shut them so that she wouldn't look back. But it was hard because she could swear she heard a little boy asking her to stay. To not leave him alone.

I can't stay. Staying with Tomas? That was crazy. His whole existence and hidden lair were crazy.

She needed to go while she could. The older lady with the elegant cheekbones and rapier gaze made an immense dragon. Not quite as big as Tomas, but impressive. Chandra scrunched up her courage and let the old lady grab her in her claws.

It proved scarier than with Tomas. With him, she didn't fear dying. Even when he'd dropped her, a part of her knew he wouldn't let her fall far.

But this woman? This woman, who obviously had baggage with her grandson? She just might for the fun of it.

Thankfully, they didn't have too far to go. The old lady flew her only as far as the car she'd parked in some lot for those who liked to hike the trails in the Rockies. The elegantly appointed Mercedes smelled of violets and mint candy.

Tomas's grandmother shifted, and Chandra averted her gaze as the old woman rummaged in the trunk of her car.

"Put this on."

Chandra caught the bundle of fabric. The tracksuit, while smelling of lavender, was a welcome respite from the robe.

She dressed quickly and stared at the majestic mountains she'd left behind, and couldn't help but track the sky for a dark speck.

"I wouldn't bother looking for Tomas. He's not coming. He always was a stubborn boy, even as a child. He also doesn't deal with loss well. It's why he cuts himself off from everything."

"Is it because of his family?" Chandra had seen the bleakness in his eyes when he spoke of losing them.

"The boy has suffered a great deal in his life. Which is why I was so surprised to find you in his aerie. He doesn't usually let anyone get close."

A part of her wanted to hold on to those words, but Chandra knew the facts. "He only took me there to protect me from Parker."

"If you say so. Still, it is odd. I guess he let his attraction to you overcome good sense. Now that you've been intimate, he's obviously come to his senses."

Chandra wanted to hide. Instead, she managed a faint, "I don't know what you're talking about."

"Don't lie to me, child. His scent is all over you."

But she'd washed.

The old lady's gaze narrowed, and then she said, as if reading her mind, "You can't wash away his mark that easily."

"I'll be doing my damnedest to scrub it as soon as I get to the nearest motel."

"Scrub your mind while you're at it. Forget you ever met my grandson."

"I doubt we'll see each other again."

"Not doubt, won't. My grandson is destined for better things than a human."

"Shouldn't that be his choice?" He'd obviously not chosen Chandra, or he wouldn't have let her go.

"Tomas will do what's good for the family, and his Sept. He just needs more time to come to that realization."

"Or maybe you should realize he's a grown man who should be allowed to make his own choices."

"You dare much with your words, child. I've made humans vanish for less. As a matter of fact, given what you've seen, perhaps *you* should disappear."

Fear stuck Chandra's tongue in her mouth. She managed to say, "No, you won't."

"What makes you think that? I have no attachment to you."

"But you are attached to Tomas, and you won't do anything that might hurt your chances of getting him back."

"On the contrary, child, I would do *anything.*" Her voice lowered. "So stay away from Tomas. I won't see him hurt."

The implicit threat stuck with Chandra as they reached a town and the old woman gave her enough money to get home. It took a series of three buses for Chandra to get back to San Francisco. Her job in the Midwest had been only a temporary contract. Her true roots were on the West Coast, and the closer she got—the less likely the chance Tomas would come after—the more she felt as if she were compressing inside her skin.

I don't want to go home. Yet where else was there to go?

The taxi spilled her onto the pavement outside her building. Home sweet home. It just never felt that way.

Chandra dragged her exhausted body into the building and took the elevator up. She offered a silent prayer—*Devi, give me luck*—as she lifted her fist to knock on the door that someone was home. She'd lost her keys—wallet, identification, everything—a long time ago at this point. Were people looking for her, or had Parker swept her disappearance under an encrypted rug?

The door to her apartment opened with her roommate letting out a, "Holy shit, Chandra. You look like hell."

"Feel like it, too," she mumbled. Or so she thought. She kind of collapsed in sheer relief and exhaustion.

She spent the next few days resting. Eating. Eating lots. At times, she felt ravenous. Other times, so nauseous she feared throwing up.

She wondered if it was a side effect of the medicine Tomas had given her to heal. The wound itself—*my gunshot wound, eek*—looked almost entirely healed, no longer red and angry, and she could poke it without it feeling tender.

More tender, however, was her heart. Three days after her escape, and she still missed Tomas.

Missed the guy who'd scared her. Kidnapped her. Stolen kisses. Made her forget her morals.

Missed him so much she couldn't deal with it and had to tell someone.

"He drives me nuts," Chandra exclaimed, the story of her incarceration and her meeting tumbling from her lips at the emergency session she'd booked with her therapist.

Who knew what Marisol would think when she heard it all? Chandra's story sounded like the rantings of a mad woman.

Marisol certainly seemed a bit dubious at first. "Are you seriously claiming you got kidnapped by a dragon and brought to his secret hiding place?"

"Yes. He's got this lair hidden in some mountain, and you can only get in with this hand scanner device. And it's gorgeous inside. It's got plumbing and everything. You'd freak if you saw it. It's like some ancient temple inside that's been converted to a modern, open loft, except there're no windows." No escape. She could have stayed there with him, hidden from the world, and learned about more of the pleasure he could offer. But instead, Chandra had left.

"So, he kept you prisoner and assaulted you."

"It wasn't assault. He asked me if I wanted

to stop."

"And you didn't stop him?" Marisol gaped.

"I know. I should have. It was wrong." So wrong. "But in that moment, it felt so good." So very, very good.

"About time you let yourself loose."

Chandra's turn to gape. "How is that a good thing?"

"Because I've been telling you for a while you need to get laid. Which is why I don't understand why you left. You obviously like the guy, or you never would have let him near you."

"I do not like him. He's an arrogant control freak. A certifiable lunatic." And she missed him terribly.

Marisol arched a brow and angled her glass, filled to the brim with an amber liquid. "What makes you qualified to say that? I am the one with a degree in human behavior, after all."

"Except, he's not human." And yes, a part of Chandra knew Tomas would be peeved that she'd told anyone about him. Too bad. Chandra needed to talk to someone, and she knew Marisol would never tell. "He's not like other guys. I mean, who thinks it's all right to kidnap a woman and expect her to be happy about it? He wanted me to show *gratitude*." She waggled her brows. "If you know what I mean."

"From the sounds of it, the only gratification went to you, so he never got anything out of it. Poor guy."

"Poor guy? He seduced me."

"And you liked it."

Chandra frowned. "You're supposed to be

on my side. Why aren't you telling me to stay away from him?"

"I'm your friend, which means it's my job to tell you to start living life. Not avoiding it."

A drink of wine didn't stop Chandra's scowl at Marisol, their meeting taking place in her friend's living room rather than the office. "I am living my life. My way. I don't need a man like him messing it up."

"You mean a man with a take-charge attitude who knows how to melt your panties?"

"Stop trying to make him sound attractive."

"Are you saying he's not? Because I distinctly got the impression he was hot."

So hot. "He might be good-looking, but he's insufferable."

"Because he reminds you of your daddy."

Tomas, with his broad shoulders, tapered waist, hooked nose, and brooding gaze remind her of the rotund and balding specter of her father? "No. He's nothing like my father."

"He's good-looking, but you can't stand him, so he must be stupid, then."

"No, he's smart." Too smart. Not just because he was a professor of archeology at a respected university in the south, but also because he knew how to handle her riposte and fling his own.

"Does he smell bad? Odor can really affect our perception of someone."

"He smells…" Divine. Perfect. Lickable. "Fine."

"So, other than his arrogance and the dragon thing—which we both know is pretty freaking hot—what is it about him that you object to? From the sounds of it, he was interested in you, and you were interested in him." Marisol adjusted her wide-rimmed glasses. She was quite nearsighted.

"But I can't be interested. You know my situation." Chandra's lips turned down.

"A situation you should have changed a long time ago."

Chandra rolled her shoulders. "I've asked." But had yet to get her way.

"Then perhaps, instead of asking, you should act. You don't have to listen to your father anymore. You're a grown woman."

"I know." She did know, but it was hard sometimes to ignore a lifetime of pushing. A lifetime of expectation. For all her achievements, her family never saw the diplomas but rather what she wasn't doing for her father, for her family.

Away from them, she did her best to forget her family's chauvinism. Away from their influence, it wasn't hard. What she didn't understand was why she couldn't forget Tomas, the man/dragon who'd let her leave. *Has he already forgotten me?*

Chapter Fifteen

He tried to forget about her. Tried so very hard. But one thing kept slapping his mind over and over.

She left. Chandra actually fucking left.

Tomas didn't know whether he should fly into a rage or…fly into a rage.

She fucking left.

For some reason, when she was given the option, he didn't think she'd take it. Why would Chandra take it? Tomas had brought her to his most secret of places.

Shared things about himself.

Learned things about her, too.

But she fucking left.

She wasn't allowed to do that.

I'm not done with her. He might never be done with her.

Ever since their time at the cabin, he felt an odd possessiveness towards her. Tomas wanted her by him, always. A part of him understood it was more, though, than the thrill of ownership. He just couldn't have said what the feeling was.

Love.

No, it couldn't be love. He didn't believe in love. Didn't allow love.

But what did that leave, because his obsession with her—three days now since she'd left—was more than simply wanting to possess her. She was his treasure. His. She belonged in his collection, never mind the somewhat dubious morality of owning a person. Tomas was having problems with thinking rationally.

She did that to him. Made him crazy.

Totally unacceptable.

So what should he do?

Leave her alone? That was what his grandmother suggested when he accepted her call later that night, an emasculated part of him wondering if Chandra was begging to return.

She wasn't.

According to his grandmother, Chandra had left without a word about Tomas. *The girl is better off with her own kind. We have our own troubles to deal with now that we've been outed to the world.*

Except, what if Chandra was in trouble? She knew more than she should, knew about Parker and his experiments. Knew about Tomas and his aerie.

She posed a security risk.

Funny how easy it was to justify his chasing after her as something he had to do for his own safety.

Once he decided to look, she didn't prove hard to find. The building she lived in was tucked on a side street on the outskirts of San Francisco, not exactly where he would have pictured her. Chandra would look so much more at home naked on his bed.

Given Tomas's need for subtlety, he arrived via taxi rather than by dragon, mostly because he didn't find it very noble appearing to be seen flying through the air carrying a satchel of clothes—and somehow, wandering apartment halls naked tended to freak people out. Something about indecent exposure.

Excuse me, there is nothing indecent about my body.

Stepping out of the taxi, Tomas paid the driver and tipped him well. A generous temperament was something he also collected. The IRS gnashed their teeth every year at his donations to charity. He stacked those receipts high on his pedestal as a show of his philanthropist nature.

Once inside the lobby—the security door only needed a hard yank to snap open—he eschewed the elevator for the stairs. In his mind, elevators were nasty death traps waiting to snare the unwary and plunge them to their death.

The stairs proved quickly mounted as he took them three at a time, and he did not huff in spite of the fact that there were six flights.

Having memorized her apartment number beforehand, Tomas didn't need to check and strode with brisk purpose down the hall.

At 612, he paused, hand raised to knock.

Knock. She'sss here. I can sssmell her.

He hesitated.

Why did he hesitate?

Surely, he didn't fear seeing her again? That was foolish. He could already imagine her overjoyed expression when she flung open the door and found him there waiting.

Or would she scowl? Chandra didn't exactly behave as expected. She had, after all, left.

Surely, she expected him to chase.

Expected him to chase…

The very idea she might have manipulated him froze him. Had she planned this?

What if she had? What if, all along, she'd left, probably cackling with his grandmother about how she'd have Tomas crawling back… Because she'd made him care.

I do not.

Then why are you here?

Tomas stared at the closed door, waiting for the real answer, caught in a complex web of uncertainty. He didn't like it one bit.

Uncertainty wasn't something a dragon should ever experience, especially not over a human.

Thump.

The noise caught his attention as he turned to leave.

Someone was inside.

Of course someone was; Chandra lived here.

It meant nothing. Probably her cleaning house or being clumsy—humans ever did lack the grace of a cryptozoid and could never hope to match the finesse of a dragon.

Thump, and a small cry. A woman's cry.

Tomas didn't think twice. He whirled and kicked in the door.

It bounced off the wall as he strode in, fists clenched, ready to mete out justice or rend his garments that he might fight in true dragon form.

And who would he fight? Certainly not the woman who was on her knees mopping up spilled food.

A woman who stared at him with round eyes

and an even rounder mouth.

"What are you doing here?" Chandra exclaimed. She stood and tugged on the hem of her T-shirt—a shirt that clung to her upper body, delineating the bra she wore. The travesty.

I can't wait to strip that from you.

He inhaled the sight of her from her tousled hair to the track pants sheared off at her knees. "You can relax. I'm here."

"I can see you're here. You broke my door."

He shrugged. "I thought you were in danger."

"You thought wrong. You can't just barge in. Why didn't you knock?"

He could only repeat. "I thought you were in danger."

"Who's in danger?" The owner of the male voice appeared suddenly—and without scent.

Tomas didn't think; he reacted, springing upon the intruder and pinning him to the floor, an arm across his neck. The other man had the same caramel skin as Chandra. He wore an earring, a thick diamond in one lobe, and sported spiked hair and rounded eyes.

"Who do you work for?" Tomas growled, letting a little of his dragon peek through.

"Tomas! What are you doing? Get off him."

"You know this man?" He eyed the stranger with no scent. A wyvern, but of which family, he couldn't tell. More perturbing, the male wore no shirt. No shirt and he was in Chandra's apartment early in the morning. "Who is this male, doctor?"

Chandra sighed. "That's Ishaan. My husband."

Chapter Sixteen

To say she'd shocked Tomas was an understatement. What she didn't understand was the rage. But the rage wasn't directed at Chandra for obscuring the truth and her marriage, but at poor Ishaan, still pinned under him.

"You're her husband." Tomas leaned low and growled.

Ishaan didn't know what Tomas was and was quite smug in his reply. "I am. For five years now."

"It was arranged by our parents," she hastened to add. For some reason, it seemed important she clarify that.

"He is your husband," Tomas repeated, and she knew it was her imagination, but she could have sworn she saw smoke curling from his nostrils. Surely, he didn't—wouldn't—breathe fire.

"Don't get too excited, big guy. We are married in name only. Personally, I prefer big, tough men like you." An outrageous wink and a smile completed Ishaan's flirtation.

Did he seriously just hit on Tomas? Chandra didn't know if she should be jealous or laugh.

Poor Tomas certainly didn't know how to react.

"How can you be married to Chandra and like men?" he queried. He seemed totally baffled.

"She's a nice girl, but I like something a little extra between the legs." Ishaan squirmed under Tomas. "Can't you tell?"

At that teasing remark, spots of color appeared in Tomas's cheeks. He sprang off Ishaan and put several paces between them.

"Explain this!" he roared as he shared a glare between Chandra and her husband.

She clasped her hands and tried not to chew off her lower lip. "As I was saying, our parents, being of the old mindset, arranged our marriage. I was really young at the time. Ishaan not much older. We didn't have a say."

"But he's—he's—"

"Gay. You can say it. It won't bite," Ishaan stated. "But I do." He stood, and the brazen fellow flexed a bit. He did possess an impressive body. Tomas didn't seem to notice.

"This makes no sense," Tomas grumbled.

Chandra's hands lifted in a helpless gesture. "It made perfect sense at the time. We couldn't get out of it, and so the marriage happened. Both of us were miserable."

"Some of us more than others, given they married me off to someone of the wrong sex," Ishaan noted.

"It wasn't easy at first. I mean, here I was, married to a man who wouldn't touch me with parents who refused to listen. As it turned out, the only person I had to talk to was Ishaan. We came to an understanding. We would pretend to be married to avoid dealing with our families. In return, I got to follow my career, and he got to follow his heart."

"And dick." Ishaan winked at Tomas. "It always knows what it wants."

"So you don't sleep together?" Tomas swung a finger back and forth between them.

"Nope."

"Do your parents not suspect?"

"Well, they have been getting on our case of late about having children. We've been staving them off with stories of my career going well and not wanting to ruin it." She shrugged. "So far, it's working."

"Maybe for you, but this is not going to work for me." Tomas appeared quite put out by her situation.

She couldn't blame him. She was quite put out by her situation, too, but didn't quite know how to get out of it. "Don't worry about my marriage. It's really not any of your business."

"It is my business because you are my business."

She wanted to say a few things in that moment like, "Since when?" and a totally irrational and girly, "Oh my goddess, he likes me."

Instead, she got treated to her husband noting the tension between them. Ishaan's brows rose. "So that's how it is. I'm surprised at you, Chandra. What happened to your morals?"

She winced.

Tomas took a threatening step in Ishaan's direction.

"You can calm yourself, big guy. I'm leaving. I can see I'm the third wheel here, so I'll leave you two to argue it out and make up. Don't be too loud and keep it off the couch. Leather stains." With a wink, Ishaan left, but the air remained taut.

"You're married." Tomas sat hard on Chandra's couch and seemed stuck on that point.

"Yes."

"I'll have to make some calls," he mused aloud.

"Calls about what?" she asked, dropping back to her knees to once again mop at the mess she'd made. Fatigue had made her clumsy this morning. First, she'd dropped her spoon. Then she'd spilled her milky cereal on her foot trying to retrieve it. But that minor disaster paled to the big one sitting on her couch. The man she thought she'd left behind.

The man who'd found her.

The dragon in her living room.

Dear, Devi. What does he want from me?

I want you.

The words were not her own, and yet she chose to ignore them. Smart people did not pay mind to stray voices. In that direction loomed madness—and heavy medication.

Noting her apartment door still gaped open, she went to it and tried to close it, but the twisted and splintered jamb would require repair.

"Top of the chain, and yet you never heard of knocking," she grumbled. She shut the door and, before it could pop open, wedged a shoe in front of it. She'd have to call someone to repair it.

The mundane thoughts only served to distract her a short while from the bigger problem still mumbling about legalities and contracts.

Chandra took a seat across from Tomas,

knees crossed, hands set primly in her lap. A lady didn't usually attend to gentlemen callers in her comfortable at-home wear, but then again, he'd seen her wearing less.

Felt her, too.

She ducked her head, hoping to hide the heat in her cheeks.

"You don't love him," he stated without any preamble.

It seemed they would jump right into it. "I care for him," and before his grumble could get louder added, "As a brother. A friend. What could have been a nightmare turned out better than we could have expected." Ishaan complained a lot, but things could have been much worse. He could have wanted to consummate. Chandra wasn't sure she would have submitted to that.

"Why stay married if you're both so wrongly suited?"

She shrugged. "Habit. Ease. A desire to not cause more drama in the family."

"Drama makes life interesting, though."

"Maybe for you." Her nose wrinkled. "I've had enough to last a lifetime."

He leaned forward. "You will divorce."

"Excuse me?"

He waved a hand. "I cannot have you married."

"I don't see as it has anything to do with you."

"It has everything to do with me. I cannot keep a married woman. It's just not done unless you're looking to provoke a duel of some sort or ask for ransom."

"The right answer is you cannot keep me, period," she retorted.

A sigh escaped him. "You are being difficult."

"I'm being difficult?" Her voice hit a high note. "You're being arrogant."

"And?" He blinked at her, not at all perturbed.

She made a noise.

"I can see you're not going to be rational. I should have known, as your scent seems a little off."

"Are you now saying I smell? Again!" She blinked at him, and the arrogant idiot did not look chastened in the least.

"No, your scent is fine. Delicious, actually." He grinned and leaned forward. "Very yummy. But it's got a hint of something different now. Some kind of tilt in your pheromone level. Whatever it is, I like it."

She held up a hand, forestalling him. "I can see what you're trying to do, and it won't happen." She clamped her lips tight.

"And what am I doing, doctor?" He said the nickname in a low, caressing tone.

She shivered. She almost melted. She held firm against his allure. "You are not seducing me."

"There you are, lying again. I don't have to seduce you. I can sense your desire for me."

"What I desire is for you to leave me alone." Now there was a whopper of a lie.

And judging by his wide grin, he heard it. "Much as I'd love to prove my point, other pressing matters need to be discussed, starting with the fact that your husband"—his lips twisted—"is a wyvern. What Sept does he belong to?"

"He's a what?" She blinked at him. Surely, she'd heard wrong.

"Wyvern, as in the progeny of a human and dragon."

She shook her head. "You're wrong. Ishaan is as human as me." She knew his parents. His grandparents. Sisters and cousins. They weren't dragons. Or wyverns, or anything else for that matter.

"Actually, your visitor is right. I'm not human." A fully dressed Ishaan emerged from his bedroom, pointing a gun. "And as for what Sept, why only the greatest one to walk this earth. Crimson."

"Don't you mean another wyvern bastard?"

Ishaan's lips pulled into an ugly scowl. "You've got a big mouth, considering I'm the one holding the gun. I'm going to suggest, if you'd like to prevent any holes in your torso, that you put your hands where I can see them on top of your head, big guy."

Did Ishaan seriously threaten? Her eyes widened. "What are you doing? You don't have to hurt Tomas. I swear he won't attack you again."

"He'd better not if he enjoys living. You are both going to behave while we wait for my friends to arrive."

"Your friends? I don't understand."

Hands laced atop his crown, Tomas appeared cool and collected. Insouciance personified in a dark knit shirt and snug black jeans. Sexy. "I'm going to take a wild guess, given what's been happening in the news lately, and guess you're working with Parker?"

Ishaan smiled. "Very good. I do work for Parker, but first and foremost, I am a loyal agent for the Crimson Sept."

"You're a bastard son."

"I am and proud of it. My real father was brother to the current matriarch."

"You mean you know about dragons?" Chandra couldn't help but exclaim. "Why did you never tell me about this?"

"Because you had no need to know. You still don't. You are merely a tool with the right genes."

She frowned. "You're talking in riddles." Chandra took a step toward Ishaan, only to have the gun veer in her direction.

"Stop where you are," Ishaan said, his eyes cold, colder even than the day they'd married.

"I wouldn't do that if I were you." Tomas spoke the threat in a low tone frosted with ice.

"You don't get to make threats, big guy. I'm in control. Move, and I will kill Chandra. My people want you both, but"—Ishaan shrugged—"accidents do happen."

"Accidents do happen, like your people sending you to deal with me. They know what I am. Who I am. Have your people sold you out? After all, you are but an expendable peon, a *wyvern*." The inflection added the insult.

Ishaan stiffened. "I am a person of import in my Sept, unlike you."

"I was more important than you the day I was born. I am dragon. But you…" Tomas gave Ishaan an up and down sweep of his gaze.

"Wyverns have always been considered disposable soldiers, especially in the red families."

The gun dipped. "You don't need both legs to serve us."

Surely, he wouldn't shoot Tomas? Chandra didn't recognize this stranger in her husband's body. "Stop this."

The gun veered in her direction. "Don't move."

"I don't understand, Ishaan. I thought we were friends."

"You thought wrong. Because of you, I've had to pretend I'm something I'm not."

"So leave, then. I would have supported it."

"I couldn't. The Sept needed me. For years, they've had me watching you, cultivating you for the day you were needed."

"Needed for what? Is this because of my research?"

"Your petty work has nothing to do with it. The experiments wanted someone of good blood and health, a virgin with a mature reproductive system."

"Virgin?" Tomas latched on to the word and eyed her with incredulity. "You mean you're married but still a virgin?" He snickered.

"I told you it wasn't a real marriage," she grumbled. "And now is not the time to mock me for it."

"Actually, this changes everything." Tomas stood straight. "I am going to assume killing him is out of the question." Tomas then proceeded to answer himself. "Of course it is. Law enforcement officials always look to the wife first. I can't have you being labeled a convicted killer. And Grandmother frowns on jailbreaks."

"Stop talking." Ishaan waved the gun. "I will shoot. I can assure you, my aim is quite good."

"So is mine." Tomas grinned, and distracted by that cheerful smile, they both missed his arm winding back and then flying forward, tossing a television remote at Ishaan.

Her husband flinched, the gun wobbled, and Chandra didn't even have time to squeak before she found herself tucked under Tomas's arm.

He raced toward the door and flung it open, his speed incredibly fast as he began bolting up the hall.

But the escape had just begun.

Ishaan recovered quickly, and she heard him shouting behind them. "You won't get away."

"I accept that dare," Tomas muttered. "Hold on, doctor. We're going to have to move."

Hold on to what? From her position, Chandra could only watch. Head dangling, she got glimpses of his black boots as he pounded the dusty carpet of the hall, the once bold pattern dulled by the passage of feet and time.

Crack.

The gunshot proved loud in the hall, but she noticed no searing pain. Had Ishaan missed? Tomas provided a pretty large target, but she'd not heard him cry out.

Tomas veered left at a T-intersection. The apartment complex she lived in was large with the hallways for each floor forming a giant letter I with stairs and elevators opposite each other.

Their exit strategy involved stairs, so she was

prepared for when Tomas partially tilted his body, allowing the meaty part of his arm and shoulder to hit the door at the end of the hall.

Cric-crac.

Another retort as Ishaan fired after them, and she almost giggled—hysterically—when Tomas muttered, "Sharpshooter my perfect ass."

Yes, he did have a remarkably fine set of glutes.

Hitting the stairs, Tomas did not put her down, and he jogged them upwards, not down.

"Why would you choose the roof? This is not a good idea," she exclaimed in between teeth-jarring jostles as he bounded up the steps.

"The roof makes the most sense. More options."

If she were a bird, perhaps, or a dragon. Given Chandra was neither and didn't wander around wearing a parachute, she wasn't as keen on this choice.

"Gravity is not my friend," she managed to stutter as he did the two flights much too quickly, hitting the final door that led to a lovely rooftop deck. Just in time, too, given she heard Ishaan yelling, "They're going to the roof." Then a firecracker popping in the stairwell.

The top of the building, though, didn't look as if it would serve them any better. Tomas emerged, holding her under his arm, looking wild and crazed.

Everyone on the roof saw them. The crowd of people. The bride and groom—the first-floor neighbors, Rory Johnson and Tania Channing—standing at a makeshift altar. There were cameras.

So many cameras trained on them.

So many sets of eyes turned to stare at Tomas and Chandra. She noted the many cowboy hats. The mustaches on a few. The rugged looks.

And then the guns came out.

Someone had invited Tania Channing's Texan family to the rooftop wedding, and by the looks of it, they didn't take kindly to men kidnapping women.

"Put the girl down," one of them stated, the massive gun surely too big for the frail hand of the old lady wearing the light mauve pantsuit.

Tomas froze and muttered, "I did not expect this."

"I tried to tell you the roof was a bad idea," she grumbled.

Bodies shifted as those armed with weapons shuffled closer. Those without guns? Ripping strips out of the bride's veil for restraints, and she wanted to laugh. No way would that flimsy stuff hold Tomas.

She tried to fix the situation. "It's okay, folks. He's not hurting me. He's saving me from my husband."

Someone muttered, "Hussy."

Chandra might have retorted, but at that moment, the door behind them opened, spilling bodies onto the rooftop. Lots of bodies, Ishaan among them.

They weren't Texan, but they also came loaded—with tranquilizer guns.

"They're going to try and take you," she yelled at Tomas.

"So kind of them, but I'm not ready to

vacation again. Don't worry. I'll catch you."

Catch me? "Tom-*aaaaaas*." She transitioned his name into a scream of epic proportions as she plummeted from the eight-story building. Since she faced upward, she got to see the blue sky above, the edge of the building, and Tomas, soaring off after her, tearing at his shirt.

Getting naked for the splat.

At least she could look at him instead of the ground that would kill her.

His eyes glowed a fierce green, his muscles rippled.

Blink.

Yes, they really did ripple, and they bulged, everything on Tomas grew in size, but he retained a man-like shape, two arms, two legs, and yet, he wasn't human anymore. His face took on an alien, almost reptilian cast and from his back...

Her lips parted. "Wings." The sound was torn from her.

His wings stretched from his back, completely separate from his arms. They fluttered behind him, snapping out into a wide fan before folding tight. Tomas arrowed down, and she couldn't help but smile.

He's going to catch me. He wouldn't let her die.

His lips flattened, his eyes widened—

Wham.

Oomph. Chandra lost all her breath as something slammed into her body, driving her sideways.

"Tomas!" She screamed his name, instead of her goddess, which might be why Devi punished her by having her caught by a reptilian creature, something with human eyes but scaly skin. Scaly red skin with mottled patches. In some respects, he resembled Tomas right now, except for the fact that he clacked his teeth at her and his eyes flashed a malevolent red.

Movies said red eyes equaled evil, in a going-to-eat-your-face-off kind of way and laugh while doing it.

This won't be good.

A challenging trill filled the air, the sound high and bright yet, at the same time, conveying such violent menace.

The thing holding her warbled in reply, attempting the same fluted speech and yet, somehow, sounding slightly off. A wyvern talking out of key.

Their flight was jostled as something impacted her captor from behind.

"Ffffucker," it hissed.

It can talk. Which wasn't as interesting as the fact that the lizard thing holding her was losing his grip.

Don't drop me.

Too late.

She was falling!

She didn't have the breath to scream and lost what little she had as her flight abruptly halted. Someone caught her. Green eyes. Tomas.

Thank, Devi.

She hugged him close. "Thank you for not letting me splat."

His chest rumbled. "Welcome." A word that warmed, but she shivered when he said, "Hold on tight."

Down. Down. Down, he dipped, his wings coasting along air currents she couldn't see but felt streaming over her face.

Buildings whipped past, so fast their windows and façade were but a blurring glimpse. She wondered that he didn't worry about hitting something, but then again, what kind of traffic would they run into in this dead space between buildings? A drone or two might catch them on camera, but videos were uploaded by the tens of thousands each and every day. Only a few ever truly stood out.

Still, though, there was something eerily exhilarating about their hectic flight. Seeing brief glimpses of them in the mirrored glass.

She wondered if they'd make the news.

Oh, Devi. Please don't let me be on the news. If her father or the family saw…

Approaching a massive building, Tomas angled sharply, pumping his wings hard to grab some height.

"Where are you going?"

"Top of that building."

"What's there?"

"A good spot to fight. It's even got a bench for you to watch from."

"You're going to fight them?" She blamed the higher atmosphere for the squeak in her voice.

"I'm going to have to since I can't seem to lose them. Don't worry. I'll handle your half."

"My half. You're going to fight all of them yourself?" She leaned her forehead against his skin, hiding it from what was about to come. "This is going to involve blood, isn't it?"

"Lots of it."

She winced.

"For a doctor, you're awfully squeamish."

"A research doctor. I deal in samples, not living things that ooze."

And in the midst of it all, he laughed. "Tell you what, doctor. How about I take care of our little friends without any blood?"

"No way you can do it," she replied as he landed atop the roof he planned to use as a battleground.

"I accept the challenge."

"I wasn't challenging." She took a step away from him and noted that he wasn't kidding. A veritable miniature garden adorned the rooftop, the grass totally fake, as were most of the potted plants, but still, it served to give the place a park-like atmosphere replete with crushed stone pathways leading to a gazebo area, which provided shade and a bench. An occupied bench.

An old fellow sat there, cigarette dangling from his lip.

"You might want to leave," Tomas advised as he seated a bemused Chandra. "This is not business humans need to see."

The old fellow ground out the cigarette and took off at a run.

A rather large part of Chandra wanted to follow. Things were about to get violent again.

And naked. While Tomas had turned on his beast mode, he'd managed to keep his pants. So why did he shed them now?

She averted her gaze.

He laughed, a low rumble that she'd come to

know but hinting at a bit of darkness. Something different and primal.

He uttered a cry, another of those odd, trilling sounds from the battle in the sky. She whirled and beheld him. A dragon unleashed and glorious.

In the midday sun, his scales held an iridescent sheen, the black almost having a rainbow quality as he shifted.

"Beautiful."

I know.

The voice came from within her mind, causing her to gasp, and then she held her breath as Tomas sprang into the sky.

He hung in the air, using only a rhythmic flap of his wings to keep him steady. Approaching fast in the bright blue sky were several dark shapes, seven by her count. And among them, one dragon.

It didn't seem like a fair fight, and yet, she didn't know what to do to help.

Unperturbed, Tomas did nothing but hover, flapping his wings enough to remain aloft. He waited until the first of the wyverns was close, and then he moved.

A dart forward and he grabbed the red-skinned guy who looked an awful lot like the *raakshas* who'd attacked her car. The legs, still encased in track pants and shoes, flailed, kicking at Tomas, but his larger dragon form didn't even flinch. He twisted the wyvern as if it were a toy and tossed it.

How's that for no blood?

The voice sounded so pleased with itself. Chandra turned away.

She understood his need to act, but she couldn't bring herself to watch. A lack of attention meant she didn't see the wyvern that snuck in behind her, close enough to Chandra that she could smell its breath, pungent with garlic.

Chandra whirled but wasn't quick enough to evade the grasping claws. "Tomas!" She shouted his name as the thing dragged her to the edge of the building. "Tomas," she screamed again as the wyvern perched on the lip of the parapet.

She looked over the thing's shoulder to find Tomas. He stood in the middle of the roof, facing off with Parker.

"Will you die like a man, without begging, or show your cowardly belly and plead for your miserable life?" Tomas asked, his voice powerful enough to cut through all noise.

In the silence that followed, she clearly heard Parker's next words.

"I'm not dying today. What's more important to you, Tomas? Revenge, or the girl? Let's find out, shall we? Drop her."

Chandra began to fall before Tomas could answer.

She closed her eyes and prayed. *Devi, save me.* Because she feared Tomas might not.

Chapter Seventeen

The choice was never in question.

Tomas lunged for the edge of the wall, ignoring Parker's mocking laughter.

"You made a mistake, Tomas."

No, Parker had. And Parker would pay. Just not today.

Tomas dove hard and fast, reached out his arms, and plucked Chandra from the air.

"You caught me," she said as she snuggled against him.

Of coursse I did. Oops, he lisped the thought at her.

"I can't believe you chose to save me over decapitating Parker."

He couldn't either. This act deserved its own pedestal for outstanding awesomeness.

"What are we going to do now, though?"

Find some pants. Because not many places would let him in wearing nothing at all. But he did know of one place in San Francisco that wouldn't bat an eye. The hotel was owned by the Silvergrace family but served any dragon with money to burn.

"I wonder what possessed Parker to come hardcore at you like that."

Not just me. Parker had moved against both

of them. Of more concern, the mangy mutt seemed to be vacillating between kill and capture. Why did Parker want Chandra?

"I wonder how many cameras have caught you."

Too many. Way too many people would see his epically public performance, done not just in the name of survival but of *her* survival.

Unbelievably, Tomas had outed himself for a woman and created a media disaster of epic proportions. Being a loner didn't mean that Tomas didn't understand the ramifications of everything that had transpired.

No amount of money in the world could hide this or sweep it out of sight. Too many witnesses to everything.

Yet what choice did he have? Chandra was in danger, and he cared about that.

He cared.

Cared, dammit.

Cared so much about the woman in his arms, who held his heart in her hands and didn't even realize it.

They landed on the rooftop of the Draego Spire Hotel. A man, dressed in full livery—dark pants, matching jacket, white shirt and tie—stood just off to the side of the large landing circle. He held a robe folded over one arm, slippers in the other.

Tomas alighted and set Chandra on her feet. She took a few wobbly steps before catching her balance. Under her watchful eyes, he tightly pulled in his essence, wound it, and condensed it until he was in his man shape and making those cheeks of hers turn pink.

Someone forgot to look away.

When she did think of it, she turned her whole body, and he chuckled as he padded barefoot out of the landing circle.

He took the offered robe and slippers. "Thank you."

"If Mr. Obsidian would follow."

"Seriously?" She snickered.

"Don't laugh. Those of us with the dark scales have to choose a name from those already inscribed, or we can marry and take our wife's name."

"You didn't marry?"

"Never plan to."

"Must be nice." The strange words had him frowning as he followed her into the stairwell that would take him to a lower floor. Only Silvergrace family members were allowed rooms on the top floors.

They were soon ushered into a lavish suite.

"Bring us dinner for four," Tomas instructed their butler before shutting the door.

"Four? Expecting company?" Chandra asked from the spot she'd claimed on the couch. She looked tired and yet stunning. Her cheeks still sporting color, her eyes bright, and her hair a wild mess.

I wonder if she'd let me brush it. He'd bet it was finer than any silk he'd ever collected.

"I hope four is enough servings. I'm hungry."

"I would have shared some of mine. I'm not all that hungry."

"Oh, I planned to eat anything you didn't, don't you worry." He grinned. "While we're waiting, want to get naked and hit the shower?"

"Are you seriously flirting at a time like this? We were just attacked. In broad daylight."

"Yes, that was a bold and unexpected move. I must give credit to Parker for taking me by surprise. It won't happen again." Tomas would be vigilant at all times now.

"What about everyone who saw what happened, though?"

"It is unfortunate. But then again, the Reds have already paved the way."

"For you maybe. You don't understand." She wrung her hands. "My family will see."

"Speaking of family. Your *husband*"—he made a moue of disgust—"seems to be connected with whoever is working with Parker."

"Did you believe his story about watching over me to use me? I mean, you'd be talking about years. That's crazy, right?"

Not for those who knew how to plan and lived longer lives than mere humans.

"World domination doesn't happen in a day."

Her eyes widened. "Is that what he's after?"

Tomas shrugged. "Perhaps. But it won't happen. And we'll kill two birds with one stone because, by eliminating Parker, we'll remove the threat to you."

"By eliminate, you mean kill Parker."

Tomas saw how it pained her to contemplate the demise of another. How did she have such a soft heart, or would a better question be, when had his gotten so hard? "I don't have a choice. You know Parker won't stop. He's in too deep now."

"I know you're right." She sighed and leaned her head back on the couch. "It just seems too crazy to even talk about killing people. As a doctor, I'm supposed to be in the business of saving them."

"And you'll go back to doing that once Parker is gone."

She just didn't know that she'd be working as a doctor while living with him. He'd reveal that part to her gently later. Tomas figured he'd soften the blow by letting her choose the city. He owned properties in several major ones. Being a professor and archeologist didn't pay much, but the trust fund he'd inherited from his parents had multiplied quite well.

"How do you propose we find Parker?"

"We don't have to. It's pretty obvious he wants us."

"I'll say he wants us, but what if he no longer wants us alive and comes after us guns blazing?"

"Then, I might get a touch angry." Hurt Chandra, and he'd truly unleash the beast.

"I saw you fighting," she said, ducking her head. "You're quite ferocious."

"Why, thank you." He liked to think he was pretty badass.

"Very scary." She shivered.

"You have nothing to be frightened of. I would never hurt you."

"Maybe not on purpose. But you saw what happened today. Are we even safe here? I mean, that butler didn't even bat an eye when you landed. I thought dragons were a secret."

"We are. Were. Even before our secret came out, though, we've always had safe houses in cities. Places where we can go and request aid."

"How could we—humans—not know all this? How could the world be so blind?"

"It wasn't. But our kind has deep pockets, and for those that could not be silenced, there were other ways."

He saw her shiver again, and he couldn't help but realize she'd spoken the truth when she said he frightened her. How to make her understand that he would never hurt her?

Perhaps I should start by being there for her when she's scared.

He placed himself on the couch beside her, drawing a startled glance from Chandra.

"What are you doing?"

"Given the number of songs that mention a man being a rock of some kind, I thought perhaps I'd give it a try."

"You want to be my rock?" She repeated it and gave him the oddest look. Then smiled. Smiled so brightly, and then tucked into him.

His arms wrapped around her, her protection against the world. Did she now begin to understand what he'd do for her? He was still coming to grips with it himself.

I'd do anything.

She sighed, the warmth of it tickling the skin under his chin. She'd anchored her head into him with a trust that needed its own place of pride in the collection.

"Are we really safe here?"

"For now." Which really wouldn't do them any good long-term.

Tomas wanted Parker to come to him, but the Draego Spire carried top-of-the-line defense systems. Its patrons were too rich and too important to fuck around.

"How is it, since I've known of your existence, and that of the other cryptozoids, that everything has gotten so violent? I mean, how did your kind ever manage to hide if this is how dragons and stuff act?"

He could understand her confusion. "This isn't how it is supposed to be. We usually live by a strict set of rules. The primary one being, draw no attention. We have cleanup crews for minor incidences, but ultimately strive for complete anonymity."

"You are failing at the whole anonymity part. It's as if no one is even trying to hide anymore. Why is that? And why is Parker so determined to push it in people's faces?"

"He's obviously got some kind of agenda." Tomas just couldn't grasp what having humanity see what they were capable of, seeing their predator side, would achieve.

Shedding blood was all well and good when it was for fun and food, but Tomas wasn't interested in starting a war with humans. Dragons might have grown in number, but humanity's population had exploded.

"What's our next step?" she asked.

"Get naked and shower."

"Separately," she added.

"Take care of some bodily needs."

"Most definitely separately."

The challenge practically begged for him to do something about it. But first, business. "We have to visit a lawyer."

"For what?"

"Divorce proceedings." Chances were she'd be a widow before long, but just in case...

"I can handle my own divorce, thank you."

"I'm sure you can, but my lawyer will ensure you get to keep the shirt off his back and everything else."

"Whatever. But you're paying for it. And I get first dibs on the shower."

Tomas allowed it, mostly because he wanted a chance to use the phone without her listening in.

He waited to hear the water running behind the closed door before accessing a secure line, although how secure it was could be debated, given that the Silvergraces ran the place.

He felt no need to temper his words to his grandmother, though. "I was attacked by a Red and some of its minions today."

"I already saw." His grandmother might sound calm, but he would wager she simmered. This kind of public display by her grandson wouldn't reflect well on her.

"It was unavoidable."

"We both know that is untrue. Had you chosen to leave the girl behind, you would not have wreaked so much havoc. Do you have any idea just how many videos of you there are?"

"How about, instead of focusing on me, we try to focus on the fact that those damned Reds had their pets attack me."

"We have been sending in polite requests for information, asking why some of their wyvern offspring were spotted attacking my grandson. The nerve," his grandmother muttered.

"I take it the Mauve Sept is not in agreement with the Crimson actions."

"No one in their right mind would be okay with this. We are going to have to act."

"You can deal with them if you like. I'm going after Parker. He's the one who started this."

"And what of after? We must still do something about the Crimson Sept. They must answer for their temerity."

They needed to answer for laying a claw on Chandra. "If I align myself with the Mauve, will you wage war on my behalf?"

"Return to the family, and I will unleash our ranks with glee. About time those upstarts were taught to respect their betters."

The shower shut off, and Tomas heard the creak of a wheeled cart in the hall—his senses were hyper-tuned since the attack. "I have to go. I'll be in touch."

He hung up and had their dinner arranged on the table by the time Chandra emerged from the bathroom with a cloud of steam, her hair upswept in a towel, and her body hidden by a voluminous, white, fluffy robe.

"Did you leave me any hot water?" he asked.

"No. Besides, I'd say you could use a cold shower." She smirked as she sat down.

"A cold shower won't solve what ails me. Only you can do that."

The blush on her cheeks was worth the cheesy line.

"I'll be back in a few minutes. Be sure to leave me some food." Given he knew things could move quickly—especially from Chandra's cool don't-touch-me demeanor to kiss-me-somewhere-lower—he chose to shower now rather than regret it later.

Contrary to her claim, the water was plenty hot, and Tomas returned quick enough that she'd barely taken more than a few bites.

Chandra insisted on mealtime conversation. "That shape you changed into today, the one in between your dragon and human. What was that?"

"A glimpse of almost perfection." It was a hybrid form that wasn't easy to hold. It required focused intent to maintain for any period of time.

"Your idea of perfection looks just like those things you called wyverns."

How to make a dragon indignant? "I am most certainly nothing like them."

"You're both lizard men with wings. Looks the same to me."

Perhaps on the outside. "Nothing the same since wyverns cannot ascend."

"What does that mean?"

"It means, they cannot go past that shape. At all. Which is odd, given they have the same chromosome strand as a dragon. But something is missing. Modern science can't explain what it is, and my research into the past says our ancestors also didn't know why there was a price to pay for a mating between humans and dragons." According to ancient texts, this wasn't always the case.

"In other words, there is a naturally formed barrier to keep our species apart," she mused aloud.

"Not all species, just humans and other lower creatures on the scale."

"So dragons can procreate with other kinds of cryptozoids?"

"Yes, but it's not encouraged, and in most cases, we are too different for it to work. But it does happen. Dragons have especially been known to have progeny with the fae, but they can become quite volatile."

"What about shapeshifters? Werewolves and stuff?"

"Those births are rare and, when they happen, can go either way, shifter or dragon, but those who become dragon tend to be weak in power. In a few cases of a mixed mating, the children end up able to shift into griffins or manticores."

"Those are real, too?"

"Just about everything you've ever heard of is. Or was. Many of the less fertile species have become extinct. It is why the Septs employ breeding protocols."

"Breeding as in making women have babies?"

"Some Septs do. Females are expected to provide at least one heir for their family name. The more dragonlings they produce, the more they are rewarded."

Chandra kept eating as she talked, absently putting food into her mouth, more than he'd wager she meant to. But her body needed it. He could see the gaunt hollows in her cheeks, the frailness of her wrists. She'd lost weight, too, since she'd left the aerie.

"If your family is really into baby making, how do you ensure you don't end up with a weak line? Do you intermarry at all?"

"My grandmother could better explain the various charts kept that allow us to see who can safely mate. And there is a lot of mating that goes on outside the Sept. Alliances are made via marriage all the time. I will add, though, that certain colors mix better than others."

"It sounds so barbaric. But, then again, as you heard, it happens even with humans. My father didn't give me a choice when it came to marrying."

"My family tried, so I walked away."

"How did that go?"

A smile ghosted his lips. "Not well, as you can imagine. A dragon of the Obsidian scale is not a common thing, so my seed is in high demand."

"So how many little Tomases are running around?"

"None." He caught her gaze. "I don't believe in family." At least, he hadn't. Then he met Chandra and was now having to start rethinking some of his positions.

"Why the breeding regime? Are you not reproducing in high enough numbers? I would have thought, as an apex predator, you wouldn't be in danger of extinction."

He smiled at her use of apex predator. "We are superior, and yet, our kind has adhered to strict breeding schedules for centuries now since the humans decimated our numbers. We got complacent and paid the price." Dragons died by the hundreds, and the humans also killed the last Gold.

Or had they? His grandmother seemed pretty convinced that a Gold was about to return. A Gold who would liberate the dragons and give them the world.

Chandra held a forkful of food midair. "Are you seriously telling me itty bitty humans went against dragons and won?"

"I should note that we were much less populous in those days. Septs consisted of dozens, not hundreds of subjects. We also played many political games." Most resulted in death. "We were low in numbers when the humans decided to come after us."

"But they didn't get you all, obviously."

"Obviously, humanity did not manage to exterminate us. However, afterwards, we were few, and we hid. We had to become accustomed to living a more secluded life." Which meant, according to his great-great-grandfather—who barely tottered down from his tower anymore—who was told by his great-times-something-grandfather that, after that dark age, there was no more braising cattle in the field and then eating them. No more raiding villages for virgins.

"Parker ruined your seclusion with his announcement." Her next words emerged slowly, as if she thought it through as it passed her lips. "But what is the advantage of outing everyone? It makes no sense. He must be gaining something."

"A copious amount of death threats."

"I'm sure he had lots of those beforehand. The man is a menace to himself and society. But he's not stupid, so why does he need you? From the looks of it, he could get all the dragon samples he wants from his red buddies."

He didn't explain that the color of the dragon made a difference in the power of the dragon. Instead, he had to make her realize something else. "Did it ever occur to you that it wasn't me they were after?" Because, if there was one thing he was sure of, Ishaan hadn't expected Tomas to show up at the apartment. Ishaan didn't even know of Tomas, not at first. But when Ishaan later exited the bedroom with the gun, he'd known too much.

Add in the fact of the many men who ended up on that first rooftop. They didn't suddenly appear out of nowhere. They were already en route, which meant they were after Chandra.

"Do you mind not squeezing me so tightly?" she squeaked.

Since he'd not realized he'd rounded the table to hug her, it took him a moment to think of a reply. "Toughen up." He eased his grip but tightened his jaw.

Parker wanted Chandra.

He'll have to get through me first.

Chapter Eighteen

Something had changed during their dinner, right after the strange out-of-the-blue hug. Abruptly releasing her, Tomas returned to eating, his expression withdrawn. Almost angry.

With me?

Did he resent the fact that his coming to find her meant he'd been caught on camera? Did he seriously blame her for the trouble that plagued them?

A knock at the door saw him rising, his eyes slightly unfocused, as if he let his other senses take over.

"It's our clothes."

How did he know? Didn't matter. He was right. He returned from a short exchange at the door with a bag, which he dumped out to reveal simple garments.

"Get dressed."

"Now? After what happened?"

"Yes, now. We need to visit my friend at his office."

By friend, he meant lawyer. She didn't know if that excited or terrified her.

She noted when she exited the bathroom that, while Tomas had donned a pair of boxers, the rest of him was bare. He held the shopping bag in one hand as he held open the door.

"We need to get going quickly."

"Aren't you dressing?" Not that she minded. He had a lot to ogle. She just didn't trust that much skin on display—it made a girl want to do things…like touch it. Lick it. Definitely pet it.

"No point in getting dressed yet." He held open the elevator door for her, and once she stepped in, he hit the button labeled Roof. A touchscreen lit up and flashed, *Authorization?* He pressed his thumb to the pad, and the doors slid shut. The elevator moved, and she frowned at him.

"Why are we going to the roof?"

"Smart girl. Dumb question. We're flying to my friend's office. It's quicker."

"In a chopper?" Something with a seatbelt perhaps? She hoped.

"And pollute the air with fumes? Nope. I've got this."

He dashed her hope. "I thought being in your hybrid shape took too much energy."

"It does. Which is why"—he tugged her into the middle of the helipad circle—"I need you to hold this."

She grabbed the bag and forgot to blink—breathe—or look away as his fingers looped under the waistband of his shorts and tugged them downward. Down his long and muscled thighs. She kept her gaze on his feet. Big feet.

He stuffed the boxers into the bag. The next time she looked up, he was dragon.

"For a guy who didn't want to be seen before, you're now embracing the public limelight."

I want Parker to notice me.

Hearing his voice in her head was freaking her out less and less. Chandra didn't want to think about what that meant. *Don't tell me I'm getting used to his crazy worldviews.*

"I don't suppose you brought a harness?" she asked.

Could dragons give dirty looks? She was pretty sure he'd just given her a dragon glare and said, with mental indignation, *You are not riding me.* Which was quickly amended to, *unless we're both naked.*

She almost blushed.

Come here. He signaled with a dragon paw the size of her head, the claws wickedly sharp.

He'd not hurt her before. She'd have to trust him again.

She sighed as she lifted her arms, the shopping bag dangling from her fingers. "Don't drop me."

The trilling sound? Definitely laughter.

He ran on two feet, clutching her close, for the edge of the roof. She forced herself to watch as the rim approached.

The leap had her holding her breath and not releasing it until his wings snapped open and caught an air current.

They didn't plunge to their deaths. Only then did she relax.

The flight proved less frightening when done without anyone chasing them, trying to kill. Perhaps that was why Tomas felt a need to roll with her in the air, spinning and whirling. She clutched at him, only to realize she'd dropped the bag.

His fault.

When they landed on a rooftop—covered in asphalt shingles—she showed him her empty hands.

"Smooth move scaring me like that. Now you have no clothes."

As he shrank, she kept her eyes trained on his face—nothing lower.

He smiled. "If you wanted me naked, you just had to say so. I would have gladly accommodated."

"This isn't funny. How are we supposed to go anywhere now? Which reminds me, where does your junk go when you're a dragon? I mean, you hear all the time about hung like a horse and elephant."

"When in dragon form, it's tucked inside."

"Like a snake."

His turn to sigh. "If you must use that as an example, then yes."

"Fascinating."

"Fascinating would be you taking my snake in hand."

"How about we go inside before some news chopper goes by and catches your dangling bits on camera?"

"I'd be more worried about drones." He swept past her, grabbing her hand in passing, and tugged her through a rooftop access door. He dragged her down one set of a stairs and then spun her before the access door to the nineteenth floor.

"So, here's the plan. I want you to go in there and find Jerrard Madison's office. Once you do, walk right in."

"Won't his secretary try and stop me?"

"Yes, she's a dragon, which is why you have to walk right by her."

"Her assertiveness isn't a reason to call her names," she snapped.

"No, really, she's a dragon, and she makes a great wall when it comes to talking to my cousin. So walk past her and right in and tell Jerrard it's a nice day to play robbers and crows."

"Why can't I just say Tomas needs you?"

"Because my way is more fun," he grumbled.

"This isn't supposed to be fun."

"Why not?"

"Have you forgotten people are after us? And you're not wearing any pants?"

"So you did notice."

She was doing her best not to, so, of course, he drew her close. The stairwell must be warmer than she thought because his skin oozed heat.

"We don't have time for this."

"I disagree." He leaned closer. "There is always time for a kiss."

"I can't kiss you while you're naked." For some reason, it seemed important she not do that. Just like it was important she keep her eyes off his nakedness—lest she be tempted.

Too late.

She pushed away from him. "I'll go find that Jerrard fellow. I'll be back as soon as I can."

"Do you like blonds?" he asked suddenly.

"What?" she asked, half turning with her hand on the door.

"Never mind. I'm going with you. I just

hope the sight of my masculine perfection doesn't incite too many lusty thoughts in other women."

"Someone thinks highly of himself."

"Can't deny perfection." He placed his hand over hers on the doorknob and turned. It shouldn't have sent such an electrical shock through her.

"You can't go in there," she whispered. Surely, he jested.

"Watch me."

The door swung open and revealed a short hall lined with even more doors. Reaching the end of it, they spilled into a vast reception room that made her very aware of the fact that she stood beside a man who was completely bare.

Head held high, Chandra strode forth, noting the hum of voices from the various receptionists and law clerks, even clients, died down until only the ringing of a phone could be heard.

"May I help you?" The little blonde behind the tall desk blinked, not once looking at Chandra because she was mesmerized by Tomas, who seemed perfectly at ease and didn't deign to meet anyone's eye. He even managed to look slightly bored.

"We need to see Jerrard Madison." Tomas didn't even have the grace to blush or acknowledge his naked state.

Chandra wanted to die. Maybe have the earth swallow her. It was possible, she'd never been more embarrassed.

Whipping her gaze away, she noted a lady wearing a gray chignon and glasses perched on the tip of her nose was the only one who didn't raise her head and ogle the scene they were making.

Chandra kept her chin high as they walked past the gawkers, right past the lady in the bun who thought to stand and object.

"Don't even think about it," Chandra growled when the woman would have grabbed her arm.

Chandra strode right into the office and slammed the door shut before whirling on Tomas and snarling, "What is wrong with you? Are you trying to get me disowned by my family?" Then again, hadn't she hoped for years they would so she could start living life her way and in the open?

"Nudity is not evil, doctor. You should try it sometime."

"I am going to kill you."

"Can I watch?" said a man with a lazy drawl. "I've always wanted to see my cousin beaten by a girl."

She whirled to see a man with golden hair sitting behind a massive desk.

"Jerrard." The word emerged from Tomas, tight and clipped.

"Tomas."

The men exchanged a brusque greeting while Chandra sought to tamp down her embarrassment, quell her anger—which she realized came more from jealousy than anything else—and take note of their location.

The office, as expected from a building filled with the attendees of law, bore a lot of wood—oak bookcases, framing a centered mahogany desk. The floors sported more wood tones with the only real brightness to the space coming from the large window behind.

"Cousin. Glad you're here. I need divorce papers," Tomas stated without preamble. "And clothes, if you have any around here big enough for me." His tone seemed to indicate that unlikely, even if his cousin seemed a match for him in size and supercilious air.

Jerrard's fine golden brow arched. "Anything else? Caviar? A limo?"

"That will do for now."

"It will cost you." The man called Jerrard leaned back in his leather seat. He looked at Chandra and smiled. "And who might you be?"

"Mine."

Startled, Chandra cast a glance at Tomas. "Was that really necessary to say?"

"Just making things clear."

"No, you're not, because you're implying you own me, which you don't."

Tomas glanced away from her to Jerrard. "Disregard anything she says. She's mine. And I want her divorced by the end of the day."

"Impossible." Jerrard shook his head. "These things take time. The documents have to be filed and processed."

"Expedite it."

"It's not that simple."

"Make it simple. What if I told you to have it annulled on the grounds it was never consummated?"

At that, Jerrard burst out laughing.

Tomas glared. "I fail to see your humor."

"Do you really think anyone would believe she's never been touched by her husband? Look at her? Can you prove he was impotent?"

"Kind of." She lifted her shoulders. "I wasn't his type."

Jerrard stopped mid-laugh. "You're serious, aren't you?"

Snapping his fingers, Tomas drew his cousin's gaze back in his direction. "Very serious, so get going on whatever it is you need to do. I want her single by the morning."

"It might take—"

"I will double your fee and give you that thing you covet in my collection."

"You'd part with it?" Jerrard's eyes brightened. "Consider it done."

After that, things moved rapidly. Clothes were fetched for Tomas—a shame because she'd rather enjoyed the view. More food also arrived because, apparently, being a dragon made Tomas hungry. Once she'd signed a boatload of documents and was falling asleep against Tomas, who'd snuggled her on his lap a while ago, only then did Jerrard say they could go.

This time, they traveled by limo, not by air. And they didn't return to their previous hotel. Instead, they were disgorged at the sweeping entrance of a lush hotel in the heart of the city, and Tomas wasn't quiet about their arrival. As a matter of fact, he ensured everyone noted them there.

"What are you doing?" she hissed when he bellowed over his shoulder at the front desk for champagne to be sent. "Are you trying to let everyone know where we are?"

"Yes. Too obvious?"

"Just a little."

"Good."

"How is that good?"

"Here's the thing, doctor. Turns out, I'm a bit of a celebrity. I'm being touted as the guy who dives off the building and saves the girl from monsters."

"What are you talking about?"

Tomas paused to pull out his new phone—courtesy of Jerrard, who had decent connections—and showed her the video. She watched it three times before she could speak.

"I can't believe your rescue of me went viral, and people think it's romantic." It was romantic in retrospect. Still…what did that have to do with anything?

"We are trending right now. So any attempt to hide is only going to have people whispering about us. Why whisper when I can have them shout?"

"Won't shouting lead Parker and his goons to us?"

"Precisely."

"You're dangling us as bait." She understood the idea. "So Parker finds us, then what? You do realize he won't make it easy. He's not going to just walk into the hotel unarmed and without backup."

"No, but he will send someone, probably several someones, and I shall follow that one back to Parker's hideout."

"What if the person won't lead you back?"

"Don't poke holes in my plan."

"But it's flawed."

"Can't you just swoon and tell me how wonderful I am?"

"Is that what all your little archeology

students do?" She clasped her hands and batted her eyes. "Ooh, professor. You're so wonderful. Teach me."

"I'll teach you," he growled as they stepped into the elevator. He stuck his arm across the door, preventing anyone else from entering, and the door closed amidst grumbles. Some cities never slept. But Chandra's grainy eyes really wished she could get some.

Tired, Chandra leaned against the mirror on the back of the conveyance. "Trending or not, you're going to lose your hero status if you keep growling at people."

"Then you'll set them straight." He slapped the stop button, jolting the cab. He then turned on her and pinned an arm against either side of her body.

"What are you doing?"

"In the movies, don't the heroes always stop the elevator to steal a kiss?"

"This isn't romantic." She might have said it, but her body certainly didn't believe it. Her heart raced, and her skin heated as he drew near. Nearer. His lips hovered just above hers.

"How can you say that? We're alone."

"I didn't ask to be alone."

"You should know by now I don't ask." He leaned in and kissed her, his lips grabbing hers and making her pant within seconds.

Where did he get this power to make her forget everything except how much she wanted his touch?

A speaker crackled. "Excuse me, honored guests. Is there an issue with the elevator?"

Tomas reached behind and slapped the button to send them moving again. They didn't stop again until they reached the penthouse level.

It took two more key card scans before they were in their room. And, what a room.

It was huge, and smack-dab in the middle of it, in front of a bank of windows, stood a huge bed on a raised dais. Talk about being on display with the floor-to-ceiling windows.

In an effort to distract herself from the main focal point of the room, Chandra moved to the windows, noting more details, such as the massive soaker tub for two, also sitting up against the glass.

Dawn had crept up during their time at Jerrard's office, the sun rising from the horizon, the orange rays bathing the city in a warm, forgiving light.

The reflection in the glass showed him moving in behind her, a looming, dark presence, his virility unleashed and intent.

If I don't move, he'll touch me.

She stayed where she was, and he placed his hands on her hips. She blocked out every voice that told her this was wrong and leaned against him. His lips buried themselves in her hair, seeking her nape.

She sighed as his lips caressed. She relaxed against him, reveling in his big frame.

He pulled her back against him, snug enough that the hardness of his erection bumped against the bottom of her backside.

She should move away.

Pivoting, she laced her arms around his neck and leaned up on tiptoe. He took the invitation and kissed her. Kissed her with masterful intent, igniting the desire she couldn't seem to stop around him.

Arousal spun hot and fast, pleasure moistening her nether parts as Chandra clung to him. They kissed. Over and over they kissed until she panted against his lips and only managed to stand because he held her.

She felt a breath-catching spasm in her sex when he sucked her tongue then twined his around hers. She could only too easily remember that appendage in other places.

She found herself pushed against the cold glass. But she didn't care, not even when he stripped her bare. They were in the penthouse suite. Who would see them but the birds—and dragons?

Let them watch. She didn't care. How could she care about anything when Tomas touched her?

Only because of his grip and the glass at her back did she remain standing. Her legs would surely collapse if she were left on her own.

He nudged her feet apart that he might better fit himself between her thighs. Then he lifted her, held her until her pulsing core pressed against his lower belly. And still, she didn't push him away. She drew him close that they might continue to kiss, their mouths slipping and sliding.

She mewled in loss when he moved his lips away then cried out in passion as he shifted his grip on her and drew her high enough to latch on to a pert nipple. His mouth tugged, and his teeth bit down. She moaned her pleasure and dug her nails into his back. Her legs, wrapped around his upper torso, squeezed tightly, pressing her sex against him, giving her enough friction to make her want to cry in frustration.

His hands had shifted from her waist to her buttocks, the large palms kneading and playing with her cheeks as his mouth toyed with her ripe buds.

She couldn't help but respond to his touch. Couldn't help but want more.

His teeth nipped her harder, and she cried out, the pain actually pleasurable, sending a quiver through her sex.

He bit again, and once more, she mewled and squirmed against him. Suddenly, she wasn't pressed against the glass anymore, but her back was on the bed, and he was kissing his way down her belly to her mound. He knelt between her spread legs, and she couldn't blush at how exposed she was, not when the heat in his gaze, that ardent desire, boiled her blood.

He used a single finger to trace the edge of a trembling lip. She couldn't help but shudder, and she felt herself getting wetter.

So wet and needy for him.

"Sweet. So sweet," he murmured before pressing his mouth to her core. He licked her, licked and lapped and nibbled.

The pleasure was too much. "Tomas!" She cried his name as her body quivered. She could feel herself climbing that precipice again, the one he'd shown her earlier, the one with so much pleasure. She couldn't wait to jump off this time.

She couldn't help but squirm as the bliss intensified. He wrapped an arm around her thighs, anchoring her in place that he might continue to spread her nether lips. He plunged his tongue inside her as she bucked on the bed, her fingers pulling at the sheets in wild abandon.

When she thought she couldn't take it anymore, he stopped torturing her channel to tease her clit. He tantalized it relentlessly, flicking his tongue across it, wet swipes that felt so good. It was going to make her come.

As if sensing how close she was to the edge, he changed tactics. He sucked her pleasure button and squeezed it with his lips.

A quiver rocked her body, and she couldn't help but beg. "Please, Tomas." She needed relief, and only he could give it to her.

She was ready.

He covered her body with his own, his lips capturing hers in a passionate kiss, his arms propping him over her so he didn't crush. The head of his shaft bumped against her sex, and she couldn't help but stiffen. It felt so big.

Too big.

She didn't let trepidation stop her. She knew enough about biology to know it would work. And she trusted Tomas to keep giving her pleasure. She just had to get over one slight little problem.

The tip of him butted against the barrier of her maidenhead, and he paused.

"This might hurt a little," he warned against her lips in between kisses.

"I can handle it." She could. She was done waiting. She was a woman, with needs and desires. A woman who wanted to finally experience life to its fullest. And that included sex, with this man, right now.

She kissed him, tasting herself on his lips but not shying away. He pushed into her, and it burned, and she cried out as he shoved past that barrier.

For a moment, he didn't move, and she realized after a few breaths she had dug her nails deep into his shoulders. But the worst of it was done now.

She shifted her hips, and he groaned. He began to move inside her, small back and forth strokes that reignited the passion that had started to slow. He tucked a hand under her buttocks and lifted her, giving him a deeper angle of penetration that stole her breath each time he butted against a sensitive spot inside.

Soon, they were both panting and rocking, his speed increasing, and in response, her channel squeezed him, squeezed him so hard.

He buried his face in the crook where her neck met her shoulder, and his lips latched on to her skin, sucking at the tender flesh over her pulse. His hips pistoned, driving him deep into her, and she welcomed it. Welcomed it and came.

Oh, how she came. Her body shattered into so many pieces as pure pleasure engulfed her and remade her.

In the midst of it, she heard him cry out; he bellowed her name. Roared against her skin and stiffened as he thrust one last time into her. But it was his bite, the sharp nip of skin that triggered her second orgasm, and for a moment, she was pretty sure she left her body and floated over it.

How lovely they looked, her tanned limbs wrapped around his pale ones.

It took several heaving moments before she regained any kind of coherent thought. And even then, those thoughts were of how nice she felt.

How perfect this was.

Lying under Tomas, their naked skin almost melded together, a happy glow permeated every atom of her being. So this was sex.

Not just sex, but mind-blowing sex, the kind she'd heard about but never believed. *This is how it should be when you love someone.*

Love?

Dear, Devi. When had that occurred? And now that it had, what would happen next?

Chapter Nineteen

What happened?

I bit her.

The throes of sex—sex he'd indulged in without protection or second thought—had resulted in a bite. Not just any bite. *The bite.*

The kind of bite that said she now belonged to him.

He chose not to explain that to her, though, when she touched the mark his teeth had left. Let her think it an enthusiastic hickey for the moment. He didn't need her getting indignant that he'd forgotten to ask about claiming her.

Why don't you ask?

Because he feared she would say no.

Even more, he feared something happening to take her from him, which was why, despite the euphoria of claiming her, he was a mess of nerves.

When would something happen? The fact that Parker and his minions hadn't made a move grated.

Tomas needed to expend some energy, but he'd already claimed Chandra more than he should, given her previously virginal state. He had to remember she was more fragile than he. She needed time to recover.

At the moment, she slept, her hair fanned over the pillow, her features delicate perfection. Her body was hidden by a blanket, but he could imagine it. Even better, he still remembered her sweet, honeyed taste.

His cock hardened, and he could have groaned.

What to do with the excess energy flooding his system? When he and Chandra had tumbled into bed the day before, they didn't leave it much except for room service and showers. Followed by acts that required more showering.

But he still had too much pent-up adrenaline. She woke and stretched. The smile she sent his way had more wattage than the sun.

He almost melted into a puddle, and then he found his balls and smiled back. So much for being Mr. Suave.

"Did you sleep at all?" she asked.

"Enough," he replied as he paced the room, wearing not a stitch. She no longer blushed and looked away. It didn't help with his permanent erection.

"Still no sign of Parker?" she asked, sitting up in the bed, a sheet modestly tucked to hide her most excellent breasts.

"Not a damned thing," he griped aloud. "We've been here forever."

"Twenty-nine hours," she corrected.

"More than a day, and still nobody has tried to attack." His shoulders slumped. Had his reputation grown too vast? Did Parker fear coming after Tomas given his abject failure before? The problem with greatness? Finding opponents.

"You'd think the fact that Parker isn't interested in us would be good news, but you seem upset."

"I am upset. What's the point of setting a trap if no one will walk into it? And don't kid yourself. Parker's not done with us. He's just waiting for us to let down our guard." He whirled, and yet she didn't notice. Didn't even glance his way, more interested in the tablet she'd snared off his nightstand. What did she find more interesting than him? "What are you looking at?"

"Just checking the news."

"I'm being ignored for the news. There is no point in my strutting naked, showing off my assets, if you're not going to admire them." How was she resisting? He was finding it epically difficult to leave her alone. He wanted to dive onto that bed, tear the sheet from her—material that dared to touch her skin. His skin. He wanted to curl himself around her and cherish her, his most precious thing.

She is better than any treasure.

Hack. He almost choked. Where had that thought come from?

"I see I'll be adding narcissistic complex to your list of attributes," she muttered, not taking her eyes off the screen. Did she not realize he'd suffered an epiphany?

She'd gotten him to care. And not just care.

Dammit. He loved her.

Shit. Shit. Shit.

How could that have happened? He hadn't meant for it to happen. And yet, it had. He cared for this woman, cared so damned much he would do anything to keep her safe and with him. Even give up his treasure.

It was a turning point in this dragon's life, and she didn't even know it.

Look at me. He pushed the thought at her.

She still scrolled the tablet. Her brow creased, and she muttered, "Later."

Later? What was wrong with now? "What is more interesting than me?" Because, really, he couldn't think of anything more fascinating. Well, there was one thing he liked more, but she was ignoring him, preferring to type and read whatever appeared on her screen.

"Oh, stop whining. You're a big, bad dragon. You can handle a little separation."

"Are you calling me clingy?" He was not clingy. Possessive and coveting were completely different.

"If I'm wearing you more hours in a day than my underwear, then yes."

He blinked. "There's a measurement for clinginess?"

"Yes, and you're coming awfully close to it."

"I'll try and be more careful."

At that, she did peek at him and wink. "Not too careful. I never said I didn't like wearing you. Wearing you is what I'm planning to do after we eat. In the shower."

"I think that can be arranged." Said with utmost seriousness, even though he wanted to chuckle. It delighted him that Chandra didn't act as expected. She didn't rush or crowd him. Didn't try and extract promises. She was her own woman. One who was with him, not out of politics but genuine desire.

He might have started out trying to seduce and own her, but in the end, she was the one who owned him.

It would sound emasculating and pathetic if said aloud to another man—*I'd do anything for her.* But it was true.

And having admitted that, he needed to do something to earn his balls back.

"If I remember correctly, didn't you tell me you were kidnapped from an archeological dig?" Chandra addressed him regarding something he'd not even thought about since their escape.

"I did." As if he could forget having gotten caught flat-footed. "Why?"

"Is this the place?" She pointed to a map on her screen.

Reading the name of the town where he'd been abducted brought a scowl. "That's the place. The irony of it was I had just about given up. Some of my research must have been really wrong because, despite the clues, none of our excavating ended up revealing anything of note." It totally sucked, as he'd been so sure he'd found the right locale. Wrong, and such a blow to his ego. He'd never found more than a few broken trinkets.

"Actually, you were almost right."

"What do you mean almost?"

"After your departure, another archeologist took over your dig."

"They replaced me?" Impossible. One couldn't replace his brand of greatness. And why would they have done that given the location proved a dud? It made no sense to have someone take over to continue searching.

"They replaced you within a week. According to the news on the net, a young fellow, a graduate from another school, approached your university. He had a theory based on your current project. The university told him to give it a shot, and the guy went on to find a ruin."

"Someone stole my glory." The nerve. Tomas had planned a lovely sandstone pedestal for this accomplishment. And another professor had swooped in and taken the credit.

"It wasn't really stealing since he actually dug in a different spot. He had to get permission from the owners of some land about a half-mile off from where you were. He landmarked the spot using some really old tree."

A tree? There was only one ancient tree of worth in the area. A gnarly olive tree thought to be over three thousand years old, even older than the one in Crete. He'd stood in front of that thickly trunked piece of history. While it didn't tower, the base of it was thick, so very thick at almost sixteen feet, and pockmarked with age. Yet it still produced the most magnificent olives because the owner of it tended to it religiously.

"There is no way anyone let him cut it down. Who would even have the nerve to ask?" Tomas certainly hadn't. The old tree was a veritable treasure of history. Tomas would never destroy something like that.

"Lightning struck the tree and felled it. The owner decided to have it carted off since people were stealing pieces of it for luck. So when that other guy went asking to dig, the owner agreed."

Probably for a price. "And what did he

find?"

"Amidst the roots, they located the crushed entrance to some kind of temple."

The temple he should have found. Another thing to blame on Parker.

"And you're telling me this to what, rub salt in the wound?"

"No, to show you that you were really close."

Nice of her to point out his coordinates were wrong. *Perhaps I should show her my navigational skills are working fine.*

"Don't pout. It's not attractive."

He pulled in his lower lip so he could better glare.

She grinned, her expression bright and full of mirth. "I'm lying. It's totally attractive."

"Then let's go have that shower now."

"Not yet. I found something you need to see."

"I need to see you naked."

"Later. Have a little self-control."

He almost whined, *I don't want to.* "I am in perfect control."

"Now who's lying?" She gazed at his erection.

He waggled his hips.

She bit her lip to hold in laughter and shook her head. "That was not sexy."

"It would have been if we added music."

Another giggle escaped her. "Nope. But thanks for the laugh."

"So glad my manhood could entertain."

"Don't pout. Come over here instead and

take a look at this."

He almost sighed. The way she held him off tested his patience. "What do you want me to see?"

"Pictures of the discovery by that other guy. A bunch of images have been uploaded. I found them when I was searching. You'll want to see them."

He would have liked to say no, but the truth was Tomas did want to see. What had they found in that temple underground?

She held out the tablet so the screen faced him. He took a few steps closer. Closer still to be sure of what he saw.

Tomas stared at the images on the screen. Stared and cursed.

"What's wrong? Because that sounds like jealousy plus something else."

"Can you blame me for being jealous? He found a bloody hoard."

And not just any hoard, the hoard it seemed of a Golden dragon because who else would collect unrelenting amounts of gold? The other colored Septs also found themselves with an affinity for certain metals and stones, but only the Golds ever collected it to the exclusion of almost anything else.

It was an unbelievable historical find. A treasure of epic proportions. But...Tomas noted a slight issue with the images. "The hoard was touched before they began documenting it."

"How can you tell?" Her fingers slid over the screen, a tap enlarging some images, a pinch and widening of her fingers zooming it. Magnified, they could make out details in the towering stack of gold—candlesticks, chains, rings, crowns, and so much more. But that wasn't the only thing in the vast chamber. It was set up to entertain, with furniture made of gold, the soft metal melted and molded into finely filigreed décor that was beautiful to look at, but he feared what would happen if someone were to actually sit on it. Ringing the room, much like Tomas had in his aerie, pedestals, each displaying a very prized item.

Draping himself on the bed, Tomas propped himself with an arm and pointed to a pair of spots in the pictures. "Zoom on one of these."

"What am I looking at?" She pulled on the pic, trying to make it bigger, but the blurry pixels made it hard to discern.

But Tomas knew what they looked at. "There are two empty pedestals."

"And? For all we know, the stuff on them fell or maybe biodegraded. They say that tree was three thousand years old."

"It didn't fall or decay."

"Then maybe it was moved, and these pictures came after."

He shook his head. "No, these pictures show the room as they found it. Go back to the search engine and let's see if there's a clearer picture."

Some people might have argued with Tomas, but in this, Chandra listened. She was curious, she had the mind of a scientist, and she liked looking for evidence.

"Here's a higher resolution one." Chandra presented a much clearer copy.

"Zoom here." He stabbed the screen, and she enlarged it. He pointed again. "See the dark crud on the shelf of the pedestal? The dust is too even for anything to have moved recently but too thin for it to have been very long. Everything else is covered in a fine silt." He indicated another section where the wall of the giant treasure chamber had caved in. "I'll bet this was a secondary entrance, created by thieves. They probably began emptying the room and would have cleaned it right out if it hadn't collapsed."

"And they didn't return?"

"Perhaps they couldn't, or they needed a better access point and had to wait." He rubbed his chin. "Can you show me the fellow who dug under the tree?" Did he know him?

A quick type of letters in a search window and Chandra pulled up a picture of a young man, his hair blond, his gaze a piercing green. He stared right into the camera, as if knowing his picture was being taken. Daring it.

Something in the face, the attitude, struck a chord. He was familiar, and yet Tomas knew he'd never seen him before. Who was this man?

"What's his name?" he asked, wondering if it would ring a bell.

"Samael D'Ore. Recent graduate. Seems to come from a bit of money."

She listed out some boring facts about Mr. D'Ore. But the only two that mattered to Tomas were, how had the man known where to look? And was the lightning strike accidental?

A suspicious mind wanted to know because he understood how single-minded and cutthroat people could be.

When an academic was starting out in the

archeological field, the best thing that could happen was finding something notable. Something of worth to bring prestige to a name. The more esteem, the better the options both for university placement and for funding when it came to pursuing his own curiosities.

D'Ore had beaten all odds. How did a human find a Golden hoard? *Is he human?*

He couldn't shake a strange feeling about the fellow.

A knock at the door had him bouncing off the bed to stand. His hands dangled by his sides, and he listened.

"Why aren't you answering?" she whispered.

"I didn't hear our visitor arrive." While engrossed in Chandra and the discovery, a part of him always remained alert. He listened and yet never got even the slightest whisper of notice that someone approached, and knocked now for a second time.

"Put some clothes on," he ordered.

He wasn't even done talking, and she was scrambling for cover. He went striding for the door.

"Tomas, you can't answer it like that."

Like what? He looked down. Ah, yes, still naked.

Too late to stop now. He'd already swung open the door.

A low whistle greeted him. "Hot dimples and dumplings, wouldn't Mother love it if I brought you home?" The woman in the doorway eyed him like a prime piece of meat, and in a sense, he was to her.

The dragonesses of all the Septs tended to

be quite marriage-minded, especially when they came across eligible dragon males. They were in short supply.

She kept eyeing, so long that he wanted to cover himself, especially when she asked, "Are you claimed?"

"I am not on the market."

"Pity. You'd make lovely babies. I don't suppose you'd donate some sperm to the cause?"

Used to the breeding bluntness, Tomas didn't flinch, but Chandra seemed upset.

"He is not donating anything at the moment. But he does need to put pants on." Chandra slapped him in the arm with the fabric of his trousers. He cast her a glance and was more than pleased to note her eyes sparking with displeasure.

Jealousy suited her, and he thought about prolonging it. However, since forbidden sex would hurt, he took the pants and turned around to step into them. It was with a wide smile he said, "You heard the doctor. I'm taken."

"That's not what I said." Chandra blew out a breath. "You can date whomever you like." She practically spat the words.

His grin stretched to face-splitting proportions. This was getting good. "I choose to date you, doctor." While Chandra mulled that over, he seated himself on the couch, crossed a leg, and addressed the silver-haired female.

"Who are you?"

"Deka, and over there is my Aunt Waida."

A glance over his shoulder showed a female entering into the room from the bathroom, her gray hair bound in a ponytail, her body clad in rappelling gear. So much for the sealed windows.

"How might I help you ladies today? As you can see, I'm not available for your pleasure."

"Your ego is stunning," Chandra muttered.

"Thank you."

"He's pretty," announced Waida. "Is he sure he won't donate to the family? We can pay."

"How about you leave?" Chandra said.

"But we haven't even talked yet."

"Talked about what?" Chandra asked while Tomas waited.

This farce still missed a player.

Knock. Knock. The raps at the door had Deka exclaiming, "About time. I swear, ever since Adi got hitched, she's been late to everything."

As Deka turned to stomp away, Chandra moved closer to him. "Aren't you going to do something?" Chandra hissed.

"I am. I'm sitting."

"Why are you acting so cool?"

"Because they aren't here to kill either of us. The Silver Sept has too much honor for that."

Having heard his comment, a returning Deka dipped her short, silver bob. "We have too much honor, which pisses me off to no end. But not as much as Adi." She jerked her thumb at the newest arrival. "My cousin hates being told no."

"When the world revolves around you, everyone should just obey." The female with short hair streaked with pink shrugged.

Deka snorted. "So delusional. The world is mine."

Even more delusional since everyone knew the universe existed solely because of Tomas.

"Now that you're all here, I suppose I should ask whether you are here on the side of the Crimson or against."

Disdain twisted Deka's features. "Are you seriously asking? That's just plain rude."

"And that answers the question. If you're not here to kill me, then why are you, and by whose orders?"

"The matriarch of the Silvergraces and the head of our Sept has sent us. Certain intelligence we've gathered gives us reason to believe an ambush is coming."

"From whom?" He had his suspicions.

She confirmed it. "The Crimson Sept, and they're not abiding by our laws. You're not safe here."

"I know. I actually hoped you were my enemies when you knocked."

"Do your enemies usually knock?" Chandra asked.

"No, but there is always a first time for niceties."

Chandra snorted. "How about today? Why do you immediately believe her when she says she's on our side?"

"You will learn, doctor, that our kind has a code of conduct. It has held us steady for millennia."

"But you said some of your kind broke that code and went public."

"They did, which means they broke a cardinal rule, and there is only one recourse for that."

"That still doesn't explain why they're here."

"The Silver Sept wishes to align with me."

Deka nodded. "We have need of you. Especially if we're to wrest the Golden dragon from Parker."

That claim didn't shock him as much as it should have. He'd been hearing about this supposed Gold enough now that he was beginning to believe it. "What makes you think Parker has a Gold? None have been seen since the wars."

"We don't know for sure it's a Gold, but we do know he's got something. Something that could tilt the balance of this world and those who control it. You've heard of his experiments."

"Yes." He didn't feel a need to explain he'd been part of them.

"I won't go into all the boring details of how Parker made a gator into a dragon. Mother is still having apoplexy over it. Needless to say, Aunt Xylia insists that for Brandon to have ascended, and show Gold attributes, he must have been infused with the essence of a Gold."

"So that's why you think Parker has him in hiding." He leaned back and draped an arm around Chandra, drawing her down onto his lap. Always best to let other predators in the room know what belonged to a man.

She held herself rigidly, and the color in her cheeks was bright. "Why are you coming to Tomas with this information? What do you expect him to do?"

"Tomas is going to lead us to him."

Sounded like an awesome plan, until the most priceless thing he owned said, "I'm going, too."

Chapter Twenty

No amount of arguing would dissuade Chandra, which meant Tomas still glowered at her from across the jet. The man sulked because she'd insisted on coming along instead of going to a safe house.

But Chandra wasn't about to hide herself away, not knowing what happened. How could she stay away from Tomas for who knew how long?

She might have teased him about being clingy, but the truth was she had to fight constantly not to throw herself at him. It baffled her how much she enjoyed sitting on his lap, snuggling as they watched television. Making love anywhere they chose.

And that was what it was to Chandra. Love. She loved a chauvinistic, arrogant dragon, who wanted to tuck her away to keep her safe. But Chandra wasn't the type to hide.

Dear Devi, I love him, but is a future with him even possible?

It'd better be because contemplating a future without him proved even more terrifying.

"You should have stayed behind," he grumbled.

"We're a team."

"More than a team, if you ask me," Deka added with a snort.

Tomas glared. Deka snickered some more. Adi was snuggled in the back on some guy's lap, and the aunt snored closer to the cockpit. The private jet came in handy when hatching plots.

As part of the ruse to bait Parker, Chandra and Tomas were smuggled from the plane to a car, careful placement of the luggage carts providing a screen.

They drove from there to the Silvergrace manor—and Chandra meant *manor*. She'd never been this close to something this big. The house had more windows than she could easily count.

"How many people live there?" she asked.

Sharing the back of the second row of the SUV with them, Deka answered. "It depends on the time of year and who's working out of town. Right now, we're a little light, given Adi and Aimi both moved out with their men."

"Your jealousy warms me," Adi replied from her spot in the third row, leaning against a big human she called mate. Chandra knew the guy. They'd briefly worked together at Lytropia, and he was who she'd called when she got in trouble.

Dex had been happy to see Chandra alive, his relief palpable, as well as his wince. "Sorry, I didn't go looking. I thought for sure you were a goner. Especially once Lytropia was destroyed."

At least he'd noticed she was gone. Her family had never even realized it. Then again, Ishaan might have lied, seeing as how he probably knew about her capture and wanted to keep it secret.

Spilling out of the SUV, she paused to crane and gawk. The giant house awed Chandra, and the outside, while grand, couldn't compare to the interior.

She loved the vaulted ceilings and the intricate plasterwork all around. While the surroundings were pretty, she wouldn't want to live here. Imagine having to dust.

A woman who'd aged with elegant grace soon arrived to meet them. "There you are, Professor Obsidian, and you've brought company." The woman's lips turned down. "Adi, please put our guest somewhere while I take the professor to meet someone."

"Who?"

"A colleague of yours. Dr. D'Ore."

"He's here?"

"Yes, and uninvited, too." The moue clearly stated this was considered quite a faux pas.

"Take me to him at once." Tomas didn't ask, he ordered.

"Deka, attend the human."

"Actually, the doctor stays with me." Tomas didn't ask; he stated. "I wouldn't want her to be accidentally misplaced."

"In a cooking pot," snickered Adi.

Having begun to get used to the rather odd humor Tomas displayed, Chandra ignored the cannibal reference. "I promise to stay out of the way unless Tomas tries to eat the guy."

"I wouldn't eat him. Too scrawny."

"But you have thought of dismemberment," she said with a tilt of her head.

He smiled. "It makes for a more permanent

death."

"And that is why I want to be cremated," Deka advised them all. "Zombies don't come back from ashes."

"They also don't taste very good." At a sharp glance from Chandra, Adi shrugged and gave a sheepish grin. "Or so I hear."

How, oh how, had these people managed to remain hidden? They gave themselves away at every turn.

Perhaps they just don't hide themselves from me. Chandra was allowed in on the secret. Problem was, would they ever let her out?

Not alive.

Gulp.

Fingers laced with hers as Tomas grabbed hold of Chandra before he followed their hostess. "Don't worry, doctor. Zombies are rare and harder to create than you'd think."

She should be appalled they even existed, and yet, the scientist in her clapped her hands and went "oooooh." Chandra liked strange things. Even dead ones.

What she didn't like was this place with all the silver accents. The women with silvery hair, the shades of it from platinum to a deep gray. The random specks of color from a throw cushion, some books, flowers, only served to highlight the stark aesthetic beauty of the women and the home.

After traversing a few gleaming halls, they strode into an office, a large one with massive French doors at the far end that looked upon a garden. Ringing the walls, bookcases filled with leather-clad tomes. In the middle of the room, a

huge desk with a chair behind it and, in front, a pair
of club seats.

One held a silver-haired woman of
indeterminate years. While her features appeared
smooth, there was a certain grace and serenity that
seemed to indicate wisdom.

In the other chair, Dr. Samael D'Ore. Just as
blond and good-looking in person, younger
seeming too as he laughed and talked to the woman
with the chignon.

"Really, Yolanda. I left you to guard the boy,
not flirt," snapped the woman that news reports
called Zahra Silvergrace. Heiress but also a shrewd
businesswoman who'd grown her empire. She took
her seat behind the massive desk, staking her
importance.

The woman with the bun waved a hand.
"The boy is harmless."

"So harmless he showed up here
unannounced asking to see Dr. Obsidian, which is
odd given his travel here was done quite discreetly."

"I have my sources," D'Ore claimed with a
smile. He stood and held out a hand in Tomas's
direction. "I'm Dr. Samael D'Ore, and might I say it
is a pleasure to meet the legendary Dr. Tomas
Obsidian. I wrote my thesis on you. I can only hope
to become as great when I reach your age."

Tomas stiffened. "I am not old, boy. And it
will take more than luck next time for you to find a
treasure. Some people only manage it once in a
lifetime."

Chandra wanted to shake her head at the
male posturing.

"I guess we'll have to see. But I do have an

advantage." The sly smile didn't sit right with Chandra.

This whole situation seemed odd. This wasn't in the plan. The plan was to have Tomas come here and for it to accidentally slip he was hiding with the Silvergraces. Being a guy, it wouldn't last. Tomas would leave in a huff, alone, and Parker would try and nab him.

"And what would that advantage be?" Tomas asked. He didn't show anything but polite courtesy on the surface, but she heard his mind-whisper of, *Be ready. He's not what he seems.*

"Whatever his advantage is, he's not wearing it," Mrs. Silvergrace announced. "He was searched quite thoroughly before being allowed inside."

"And yet you missed it." D'Ore shook his head. "Perhaps you should look again."

Tomas canted his head and stared at D'Ore as if he could see what the man hid by pure force of will.

Undaunted, D'Ore stared back, the faint hint of a smirk on his lips. "Have you figured it out yet?"

"You're not human."

"What are you talking about?" Yolanda frowned. "Smell him. It's quite distinct."

"It is," Tomas agreed. "Did you know Parker's been working on a formula at his labs to mimic human smell and hide dragons?" They'd tested it on him.

"Someone needs to eat that man," someone muttered.

Tomas moved closer until he stood right behind D'Ore. The man didn't turn to watch but rather looked straight left, his piercing gaze stuck on Chandra.

"If it isn't the missing doctor. I hear your disappearance caused quite the ruckus."

"What are you talking about?" Tomas growled as he rounded the chair and loomed in front of the young man. "What do you know about Chandra?"

"More than I wager you do. For one thing, I know Parker wants her back."

"The human girl? Why?" This came from Mrs. Silvergrace.

"She's part of the plan. So are you, Tomas." D'Ore took a step forward. "The time is coming. Things are moving into place. Will you be with or against us in the final battle?"

Who is us? Chandra wondered. She blinked before she'd even formed a reply then completely lost the thread as chaos erupted.

"Where did he go?" Yolanda exclaimed.

"He was right here. How did he vanish?" barked Mrs. Silvergrace.

"That is a cool trick," muttered Tomas.

Standing from behind her desk, the leader of the Silver Sept slammed her hands on the hard surface of her desk. "Someone get Varna and Valda to pull up the security cameras. I want to know what happened. Where did that boy go? How did he manage to disappear?"

They never did find out because, no matter how many video feeds they checked, D'Ore never appeared. As a matter of fact, it looked as if they conversed with thin air.

Adi was especially intrigued. "It's as if he

was invisible to the video recorders."

Since video looked for how light bent in respect to objects, Chandra mused aloud, "He's obviously letting light through his body rather than reflecting it back."

"Some kind of cloaking device. But the question is, was it manmade or inherent? I've never seen anything like it."

"Perhaps we should focus less on the fact that he has no reflection like a vampire, and more on that Parker wants Chandra." Tomas didn't seem the least bit impressed with that fact.

But it was Xylia, who'd just walked into the room, who had an answer. "Of course Parker wants her. Given you're sleeping together, I'm going to wager he's interested in the baby."

Thunk.

Tomas hit the floor hard.

Chapter Twenty-one

"He fainted."

Men didn't faint. Tomas merely kept his eyes closed, mostly because he didn't want to deal with reality.

Because reality sucked.

It kicked a man in the balls and then choked him of all breath.

Reality hurt his chest.

Hurt so badly.

It couldn't be true. Chandra, pregnant? Impossible. They had just slept together. Women did not get pregnant that quickly.

And, yes, he knew how pregnancy worked. He knew he could have inseminated her that first time they were fully intimate. But really, what were the chances it happened then? After that, he'd been careful. Always spilling outside her. Conscious even during pure bliss of how easy it would be to slip.

I should have used a condom.

He should have, but thoughts about a condom wouldn't erase the fact that Chandra was pregnant, pregnant long enough for her to exude a certain scent that the dragoness noticed, which meant there was no way the baby could be his. Because she'd always smelled that way to him.

Upset at the thought—*the lies, she lied to me!*—Tomas brushed past everyone in his way.

Chandra reached out to him. "I didn't know. I swear. I didn't. This can't be happening."

The pain in her voice almost sent him to his knees. Showed that he cared.

Never. The pain did serve to remind him, though, of why he had his rules. Caring always hurt.

"Leave me alone!" he barked as he strode away from her. *Leave me alone to my pain.*

Tomas stomped out of there, ignoring her soft sobs, wanting to sob himself as he tried to make sense of the fact that Chandra was pregnant.

But how? She was a virgin. He'd swear to it. He'd been the first to claim her as a man claimed a woman.

He stripped down as he pondered. Stripped and changed before taking to the skies with an ululating shriek.

Was the whole virgin thing fake? It seemed so improbable. After all, who went so far though as to have skin and blood implanted to fool him into thinking she was a virgin? He didn't care if she was, so why pretend?

It was real. And he was being ridiculous. Chandra had never been penetrated by a man before him. He'd swear it.

Then how could she carry a child? There had to be a logical answer.

Before being captured, she'd claimed to work long hours at Lytropia Institute. Then, once Parker got his hands on her, she was kept sequestered in the hidden lab. But how long was she kept hidden?

He still recalled her surprise when they escaped and she realized more time had passed than she'd guessed. A few days, at least. So many things could have happened during that time. Parker had shown he would do anything to anyone. Had he experimented on Chandra?

Did the result lie in Chandra's womb?

It was possible. All it would take was artificial insemination. Parker wouldn't have hesitated to do such a thing, and wasn't it Ishaan who had said Parker had groomed Chandra as a host for babies?

The woman he'd claimed, the woman he'd been obsessed with since meeting, the woman who unleashed the protective lover in him, was pregnant by a madman, and he'd left her alone.

Alone and crying.

In a house full of dragons—who sometimes had strange cravings.

He'd left her with strangers to protect her.

Left her alone, knowing that this D'Ore fellow seemed capable of disappearing at will. And he did it in broad daylight. Tomas could only use shadows to conceal himself.

I am a fucking moron. He'd let the initial painful shock send him fleeing. Such a big, bad dragon. Not.

Time to man up and stop running.

He banked and turned around, pumping his wings hard to bring him back to the Silvergrace mansion.

He'd no sooner landed than Deka jogged up to greet him. "There you are. I figured you'd come back soon. It worked."

"What worked?" he asked as he yanked back on the pants he'd hastily discarded.

"Your hissy fit. As soon as you stomped off, acting as if she'd done some horrible thing, the doctor asked us a few times if we were sure. Babette managed to procure a stick to pee on—which sent her mother into a fit because, hello, what does Babette need a pregnancy test for? Anyhow, the doctor peed on it and proved she was definitely preggers. I mean that stick lit up so quickly, Aunt Yolanda thinks it might be twins."

The chattering only served to irritate. "I get it. She's pregnant."

"Yes, and she's not happy about it. According to Aunt Waida, she said something rude in Swahili and then took off."

"Took off? How?"

"She called a cab and took off. Without even saying goodbye." Deka shook her head. "Humans can be so rude. But then again, it probably was for the best."

No, it was not for the best, because Chandra wasn't here. "Where did she go? I have to find her before Parker does."

"Too late for that." Deka pointed to her phone. "He got her like a few miles down the road. But don't worry, he hasn't removed the chip."

Ah, yes, the chips they'd had installed while they were on the plane just in case someone thought to steal them again. Except, when they'd had it done, Tomas expected to be the bait taken, not Chandra.

Beep. Beep. Beep. The little dot pulsed red on the map, moving away from him.

Taking Chandra away from him. His blood pressure rose.

"Want to bet this is going to lead us right to Parker?"

Who cared about Parker? Tomas needed Chandra back. Now, before he unleashed his dragon and laid waste to the world.

Chapter Twenty-two

What in the world is going on?

Chandra certainly didn't understand. She'd fled the Silvergrace mansion in a daze, trying to come to grips with the fact that she was pregnant. Struggling even more to deal with the fact that Tomas had stormed out—left because the baby wasn't his.

Dear, Devi, she didn't even know whose baby it was, but now all kinds of little things made sense from her finicky stomach to her fatigue. She could also pinpoint when it had happened—during those days she'd lost after getting caught by Parker's *raakshas*. He'd done something to her. Implanted her with what? Someone else's egg? Had he used her own? Fertilized with whose sperm?

Devi help her, what kind of child did she carry?

She couldn't help but shiver at the thought of something perhaps not entirely human nesting within. Something that could hurt her?

No. She couldn't think like that. Wouldn't. *I'm pregnant.* She placed a hand on her stomach. *No matter what, this is my child. Mine to protect.*

She just didn't know how to do that when she couldn't even save herself.

Once again, Chandra was a prisoner.

In a cage.

A real cage.

A cage inside a room furnished with too much medical equipment. That just screamed danger. The room appeared empty of anyone else. However, given the stools and the hooks by the door where a lonely sweater hung, she could assume someone would come at some point.

What did they want with her?

Nothing good, that was for sure.

I'm such an idiot. Why did I run away? She could only blame herself. When she'd called the taxi to get her out of the Silvergrace mansion—*I had to leave. Tomas was gone, and I was alone.* Alone, shocked, and scared. She'd had only one thought—escape.

But she didn't make it far in the taxi before it slowed down and her door was yanked open. She didn't even have time to protest. She didn't even get a clear view of her attackers. The dart with its drugging agent hit her too quickly.

She'd woken up here, a prisoner. She had a hysterical urge to find a cup to drag it along her bars and scream for help. But who would hear her?

Who would care?

The only furniture in her cell was a bed. A cement platform with a foam mattress on top. Chandra lay on it, facing the far wall and staring blankly. She curled into a ball as she stressed about what would happen next.

What is Parker going to do to me?

"I brought you some food." The soft voice saw Chandra rolling so fast she almost fell off the bed. She caught herself and noticed she had company in the form of a blonde girl. She was young, a teen Chandra thought at first until she truly looked at her.

The long blonde hair and unmarked face indicated youth, but the maturity of her body and features put her at someone college-aged, in her twenties.

Chandra looked at the thick and creamy soup in the bowl that the young woman passed through the bars, and her stomach churned. "I'm not hungry."

"You have to eat. For the baby."

"What do you know of the baby?" Chandra scrambled to her feet and hit the bars, grabbing them in fingers that white-knuckled.

"All I know is Uncle says you're pregnant."

"Uncle? As in Parker?"

The girl nodded.

"You should ask your uncle why he thinks I'm pregnant since I was a virgin up until two days ago." Chandra couldn't help but color her words with bitterness, and the young woman's tentative smile drooped.

"I don't know anything about that."

"I should hope not, dear niece, since you're not married. I must admit I'm shocked by you, Chandra. I thought your morals a little more firm." The devil strode in, Parker's smile wide and unrepentant. Why should he care? He had it all. He wasn't even horribly ugly.

"I should have known you were behind this," Chandra hissed.

His lips pulled into a small smile. A man in his late forties, Parker sported specks of gray in his hair and a flinty gaze that showed no mercy. "I see you've met my dear niece, who, I might add, isn't supposed to be down here. Sue-Ellen, why don't you be a darling and run along while I entertain our guest." When the girl hesitated, his tone took a deeper tone. "Now."

At the warning implicit in the word, Sue-Ellen didn't even spare Chandra a second glance before fleeing.

Lucky girl. Chandra would have liked to follow, but the whole cage thing made it kind of difficult. "You need to release me at once. Kidnapping is a federal offense."

"As is genetic experimentation." Parker took a seat on an empty stool by a barren metal counter. "Did you know I have evidence showing some questionable and unethical practices by you while working for Lytropia?"

"I never did anything wrong." A vehement denial.

He leaned forward. "But I can make it seem like you did."

"Are you threatening me?"

"Only if you force my hand. But that's not why I brought you here. You, unfortunately, left our care earlier than expected. We weren't quite done with you."

"Oh, I'd say you did enough. I have you to blame for this, don't I?" Chandra placed a hand on her tummy, still trying to come to grips with the idea that life grew in there. *My egg and someone's seed.* Whose seed?

No wonder Tomas was so angry.

"You are carrying a miracle of science. Or, at

least, it will be once I'm done with you."

"I am not some kind of lab rat you can use to advance your sick experiments. We're done."

"We'll be done when I say we're done. You and that baby are going to make history."

"I won't help you."

"You don't have a choice." His lips quirked. "How ironic that the doctor who once studied is now the subject under observation. It will give you a new perspective. And mayhap, if you behave, you can even be a part of this life-changing endeavor."

"You are utterly insane. You can't experiment on people."

"What you mean is I'm not supposed to because, I'll tell you right now, I can. And it works. You'll see."

Her mouth gaped, the claim calmly spoken, so believable.

So very frightening. He grabbed the bowl that his niece had left behind and offered it. "I see you didn't eat your soup. You really should. Must keep up your strength."

"Eat it yourself."

"Now is that any way to speak to the man who holds your life, and that of the fetus, in his hand? Eat."

She shook her head. "I'm not hungry." Not yet, but how long could she resist?

"Always with the resisting. Why is it people never understand that they're going to lose? I am in control here. I am the one who says what's going to happen, and I say you are going to eat the soup."

"I will not. And you can't make me." Chandra heard the mistake the moment she said it.

"Can't?" Parker's brow raised. "Guards." Parker raised his voice slightly, and a pair of burly men entered. "My guest needs to eat. Please help her."

"No." She backed away from the cage as a key was inserted and a door in it opened. "You can't do this." Chandra slapped her hands over her mouth, but the goons easily pried them free, and then one held her jaw open and began to pour the soup. She could drown or swallow. There wasn't any choice. So gasping and choking, tears streaming down her cheeks, she swallowed the thick soup, wondering what Parker had put in it. Convinced she felt her throat closing. Did he poison her? That would make no sense given the trouble he'd gone to in order to bring her here.

Logic didn't do a thing to quell her panic as she was forced to eat the entire contents of the bowl.

When it was gone, Parker snapped his fingers. "You may leave now." The goons left, and Parker leaned back, a self-satisfied smirk on his face. "Consider that your first lesson in obedience. You will learn to listen. Or don't. I have methods to cure that."

"You won't hurt me." Chandra didn't think Parker would harm the baby, which meant, for the moment, he wouldn't hurt her.

"Do you really think that pain is the only way to make someone bend? I have the power." He crouched down and held her gaze, a gaze that wobbled and tripled.

Something made her hazy.

Parker crooned. "I don't have to touch you

at all to take away all hope. Hell, you don't even need to be conscious to have this child. Imagine waking up in time to see the baby born. See, I don't need you. The child is what I'm after."

"Whose baby is this? Yours?"

"Mine?" He laughed. "No. My seed wasn't right for this project. We needed someone with the right kind of genes. Would you like to know who the father is?"

Yes. No. Yes.

She didn't reply, but Parker leaned close anyhow to whisper one word. A name.

Forget speaking. Stunned, she could only blink at the four smirking versions of Parker.

Her stomach cramped. She tucked her knees close.

"Nothing to say? I'm shocked. Just shocked." Parker stood. "I always liked you, Chandra. You have incredible genetics. And just think, your child will be the first. The example we will use to draw the others."

"First what? What are you planning to use my baby for?" She might not understand how it had happened, or like it, but whatever baby grew in her stomach was hers to protect. She cradled the still-flat plane of her stomach with her palm.

But he didn't reply, and her eyes blinked shut. Everything spun. Even the floor she lay on felt as if it moved. She remained flat on it, trying to regain a sense of balance.

The sharp *clack, clack, clack* pounded into her head. And then it was a melodious voice talking. "I assume you've given her the final dose." Spoken low and sultry, and rubbing all over. But the words...

The words were wrong.

"Yes. The process is complete. Now we wait for the fetus to mature."

Me? They're talking about me.

She pushed her eyes open, the lashes suddenly so heavy. Concrete eyelashes. Someone had cemented them.

Panic hit her for a moment. Then sanity reared its head.

You've been drugged.

So drugged she couldn't lift her head, but she could peek ahead and saw a few sets of feet as she did. Long, gray trousers over leather loafers. And heels. Bright red heels.

"My darling queen. You do me honor visiting."

She didn't see it but heard the loud smack of lips hitting skin.

"I heard the girl was recaptured and came to see her for myself."

"She's in our care again, and in fine health."

How could he say that? Her mouth felt as if she'd been deprived of fluids. And Chandra's head had rocks inside.

"We are sure the pregnancy took?" The woman crouched, her red sheath of a dress pulling up over lean thighs. She didn't just crouch, though; she studied. Sniffed the air. The woman's eyes sparked with green fire, and she did a disturbing lick of her lips.

As if I look delicious. Chandra held her breath as the realization hit that this woman was dragon. Judging by her words? Not a very nice one.

"The subject's womb is quickening," Parker assured.

Subject. Wince. Chandra blinked, and her lashes cooperated.

"How long until we're sure it succeeded?" The lady with the alabaster skin and vivid red hair in a chignon stood, leaving Chandra with a view of those red heels and slender ankles.

"We won't be sure until after the birth."

Nails scraped across the surface of the table, a discordant sound that made Chandra wince.

"I can't wait that long. Things are moving rapidly. We need something to stem those who are moving against me." The woman Parker called queen stood very close to him, their shoes almost touching.

"I think I have an idea. Let's speak somewhere more private."

The feet left her line of sight, and she heard the soft click of a door closing and the more ominous *thunk* of a lock engaging, leaving Chandra alone.

The initial effects of the soup appeared to be wearing off, but that didn't mean Chandra didn't act. It took some trembling, but she managed to stick a finger down her throat and gagged as she tried to force herself to vomit. She wanted that soup out of her.

It didn't work, and she collapsed, panting. The concrete floor smelled of bleach. So clean. Was it to hide what they'd done before?

The lock clicked. Someone came. Devi help her. She wanted to be brave. She really did but...she was so damned scared.

The door opened, and she could see the crack, see the booted feet that approached.

And now her stomach did heave on its own, but nothing emerged. The dry retching only served to hurt.

It also embarrassed as the boots stopped outside the cell. Someone watched her.

"Is that an indication of how happy you are to see me?"

"Tomas?" She opened her eyes and turned enough to see him, a big, blocky shape that wavered in and out.

"I'm going to get you out of there." He growled the words, and his eyes glowed with green fire. He yanked on the door to the cage, and when the lock held it shut, he grumbled louder. The muscles on his arms bulged, his face took on a stern cast, an almost alien feature, and for a moment, she could have sworn she saw ebony shadow wings behind him.

Metal screamed as it twisted, the cage no match for an angry dragon.

He dove into the cage and dropped to his knees. In mere moments, she found herself cradled in Tomas's arms.

"How did you find me?"

"Microchip."

"You mean Parker didn't disable it?" Her mind began stuttering into working mode again, the fuzziness and the stomach pains fading. With every blink, her mental acuity returned, and the questions started. "There's no way Parker wouldn't have checked me for a chip."

"Maybe he forgot, or someone didn't do

their job."

"How much resistance coming in?" she asked, her teeth gnawing at her lower lip.

"Some. Nothing I couldn't handle." Said with an arrogant grin.

"In other words, too easy."

"I wouldn't say easy. This past day, while we were apart?"

"Day?" Chandra had thought herself asleep for only hours.

"I wanted to get here faster, but we did need to prep for the visit. Lucky us, Parker practically invited us in."

"What do you mean?" she asked as she managed to lift her head and see only one Tomas.

"What he means is Parker has called a press conference. As such, his security was not as stringent as usual." Zahra Silvergrace swept into the room, a cool breeze of elegance in her silver-threaded pantsuit.

"What are you doing here?" Chandra blinked. "You shouldn't be here. It's dangerous."

Both Tomas and Zahra answered with bright smiles and an enthusiastic, "Yes, it is."

The head of the Silver Sept waved a hand. "But what is danger when a lesson must be taught? We cannot afford to look weak in front of Parker. The man is entirely too convinced of his invulnerability. It is time he was shown his proper place in the chain. Not to mention he needs punishment for his lack of decorating sense. Ostentatious place above us. All those colors." She shuddered.

"We're in Parker's house?"

"Under it," Tomas corrected as he stood with her. He kept one hand on her waist to steady her.

"And he's invited the media. That seems odd."

"It's probably a trap." Tomas grinned. "And I totally walked into it."

She blinked, but he still had that stupidly male smile. "This is not a game. Parker forced me to eat the soup."

"Hey, I take offense. What's wrong with soup? I happen to enjoy a hot bowl of it, especially during the chilly months."

She poked him in the ribs. Hard. "He put something in the soup. I think it's meant to affect the baby."

At the word baby, he swallowed hard. He turned her that he might look upon her. His expression turned flinty. "I promise we'll make him tell us what he's done and handle it."

"We?" He'd referred to them as a pair. As in a…couple?

"Yes, we. I seem to have added you to my collection."

"What do you mean added? I'm a person. You can't add me to anything."

"Actually, I can. I'm a dragon, and it seems you belong to my hoard."

"And if I refuse?"

"You can't refuse," Zahra interjected. "The man has mated you."

"Mated me?" Chandra's hand went to the bite mark on her neck. "What does that mean?" A hopeful part of her fluttered, but the more realistic part held tight and wouldn't let it fly free.

He shrugged and, for once, looked sheepish. "We are mated. I've claimed you. For life."

"Unless he trades you," Deka piped in as she sauntered into the room. She looked quite elegant in her silver sheath and heels. She studied the fingers on one hand. "I broke a nail. And I just had them done. Damned guard." She scowled.

"Language."

"Sorry, Auntie."

Chandra began to wonder if she was on some kind of reality show because, surely, all of this wasn't happening.

"Report," Zahra demanded.

"There's just this one basement level. She's the only one in a cage. The others are empty."

"Staff? Guards?" Tomas asked.

Deka shrugged. "Not as many as you'd expect in a place like this. Maybe Parker cleared them out ahead of the news conference he's holding."

"Chandra is right. This is too obvious of a trap. Which means we're not seeing something."

"Or we're doing exactly what he wants," Chandra interjected. "You shouldn't be here."

"No way was I letting you go."

The lowly growled words startled her. She didn't have time to process them.

"Does it really matter?" Deka asked. "He obviously wants us to take Chandra. And that is why we're here. So let's stop being peeved that things were too easy and go get drunk somewhere and start a bar fight."

Zahra sighed. "You are so like your

mother."

The cringe could almost be heard. "Don't say that," Deka gasped.

"If Parker wanted me to have you, then why not just give you back? Why make us come get you?"

Zahra eyed Chandra. "Are we sure she's not working for Parker?"

Before Chandra could exclaim her indignation, Tomas jumped to her rescue. "Chandra is not working for him. And whatever is going on might be related to whatever is happening above us. Or have you forgotten the last few times Parker held news conferences?"

Chandra doubted anyone would forget. The first one Parker did had revealed shapeshifters to the world. The moose memes were particularly clever.

"Most folks seemed to think the action would happen at eight."

"What time is it?" Parker asked.

Nobody looked at their wrists, as the three dragons in the room said, "Hammer time."

And one muttered, "I wish I'd brought my MC Hammer pants."

I'm surrounded by lunatics.

But lunatics who gave enough of a damn to come after her and rescue her from Parker.

As Tomas carried her down the hall, she noted she wore a plain gray tracksuit. Her feet clad in soft wool socks. Not naked, and yet, she certainly felt self-conscious as they made their way up the single hall, many of the rooms visible via viewing glasses.

Lots of empty spaces with medical equipment.

Where are the doctors and patients?

"And why is it so easy?" Tomas murmured, his arm still firmly anchored around her waist, even if she was capable of walking.

"Are you mind reading again?"

"I can feel your tension. You're worried."

"Aren't you?" she asked. The Silvergrace women weren't. They sauntered through the space as if they owned it. Arguing as only family could do.

"Worry is for those who fear destiny."

"That's just a pretty way of saying hold my beer and watch this."

"I'm more of a cognac kind of guy."

The elevator opened with the swipe of a pass Deka had filched off a guard. She'd left him sleeping off his concussion in a closet.

Only silence without the aid of music filled the elevator car on the short trip up. The doors spilled open into a small confined room with a snoring guard.

Outside that room, a wine cellar, the door to the elevator camouflaged by a swinging rack filled with bottles.

"This is right out of Scooby Doo," she remarked as it shut behind them with hardly a push.

"And see, for me, that's the norm. Because my kind has so many secrets, clever hiding places and methods to protect them are something I know a lot about."

"All dragons protect their hoard," Deka added. "It's our thing."

"And everyone has one?"

"Any real dragon does."

Deka scouted ahead while Tomas remained with Chandra, and Zahra arrived late behind them. They emerged up a set of stairs into a kitchen.

The staff dressed in white layered with white aprons didn't even look in their direction as they prepared platters of canapés and loaded trays with drinks.

Deka had quickly traversed and poked her head through the swinging door. She pulled back and shot them a look. "Seems like there're lots of people out there. Whatever it is, I don't think we've missed it."

"I swear, if that man reveals one more...." Zahra swept out of the room, taking her threat with her.

Chandra hesitated, feet rooted. "You said I'm part of your hoard. Does that mean you could trade me?"

"Not fucking likely." He sounded most indignant. "One doesn't get rid of perfection."

"But I'm pregnant. I won't stay perfect."

"So what? You're mine." The possessive claim warmed.

It didn't mean she didn't tease him. "With those words, you really prove how prehistoric you are. You're not a dragon. You're a dinosaur with longer arms."

His eyes widened. "Did you just compare me to a T-Rex?"

"Would it help if I said you were my T-Rex and I don't mind you claiming me?"

Smugness shone in his smile. "I knew you liked me."

"I shouldn't."

"But you do."

"A little." She shrugged. "Maybe a lot."

"Excellent. That means I won't have to explain how the universe works."

She blinked. "You lost me."

"It is a well-known fact that the universe revolves around dragons, more specifically me at the moment."

"You?" She laughed. "You might want to revise that opinion, dear Tomas, because, according to Parker"—she placed his hand on her belly—"this miracle of in vitro science is..." She paused before dropping the bomb. "Yours. *Daddy*."

Chapter Twenty-three

Daddy.

The word hit him harder than the floor. And no, he didn't faint. He merely rested his face on the ground for a moment.

It didn't make the room stop spinning.

All of his world spun because Chandra carried *his* child.

It occurred to him to refute it. To demand a test. To deny, deny, deny.

Except…

Deep down inside, real deep, he knew the truth. *The child is mine. Mine and Chandra's.*

The how was probably simple. During one of his fugue states, Parker had managed to take something precious from Tomas. Something more than just blood or tissue.

That seed now grew in Chandra. *I have a family.* A family that needed him. His heart palpitated with excitement. It didn't last, as his blood suddenly ran cold. Tomas remembered what Chandra had said about Parker forcing her to eat something.

What did he do to my mate and child?

Hadn't the man done enough already?

I've had enough of his games. Tomas slid an arm

around Chandra's waist before leading them from the kitchen to the dining room, their steps down as they approached the large arch leading to the front of the house and main hall. The closer they got, the louder the hum of voices.

It seemed a great many people had shown up to visit Parker. Not all of them human. His nose twitched as he noted dragon in the mix, shifter, even some Fae. Of more concern, he also scented nothing—the wyverns he brushed past made no attempt to pass themselves off as anything else.

Only a few people sent a glance Tomas's and Chandra's way, their focus more on the staircase, the kind of sweeping, fancy affair meant to present a grand dame or, in this case, a man with delusions of grandeur.

People milled around and talked, the soft buzz filling the vaulted room that served as an oversized antechamber. None of them knew why they'd been called, but excitement bristled.

"What do you think he's going to say?" Chandra asked as Tomas slowed on his way to the front door and freedom.

"I don't know, but given Parker's history, I doubt it's anything good." Tomas frowned, his dark brows knitting tightly as he looked around. "A good portion of the crowd is made up of reporters. I see a few cameramen. And that woman in the green pantsuit does the local evening news."

"A bunch of reporters in one spot?" Chandra straightened. "I think it's time the world heard about the real Parker."

"Don't fool yourself. The world knows and chooses to ignore. Parker's got deep pockets and dangerous alliances."

"So how are we going to stop him?"

At that moment, there was a stirring in the crowd.

Parker emerged at the top of the stairs on the bridge formed where the left and right met. He held his hands up, and the room quieted.

"Thank you for coming. I'm sure you're quite curious as to why I've asked you all here."

"Are you going to prove the existence of aliens this time?" someone shouted from the crowd.

"Everyone knows aliens don't exist," Parker replied with a snicker. His voice projected, whether by magic or device, it didn't matter. Everyone could hear him.

"I have called you here because I have a grand announcement. In this very house, I have the biggest secret, and I'm going to—"

If Tomas had blinked, he wouldn't have seen it, a blurring glimmer of movement, something behind Parker.

Something that pushed.

Gravity loved a good shove. Parker went sailing over the railing.

A single scream sounded out, "He's falling!"

The words no sooner rang out than it was over, the hurtling body moving too quickly to catch. Everyone heard the sound as it hit the hard, stone floor.

Crunch.

A half-second of utter shocked silence then…

"Oh my gawd, he's dead."

Parker had fallen from the top of the stairs.

And, somehow, no one could explain how it had happened.

Not even the cameras.

As for Tomas…had he seen something?

Did it matter?

His nemesis was dead. The saddest part about that was Tomas didn't get to deliver the blow.

He might have felt gypped. Except it meant, once the police were done questioning the guests who had witnessed it, he and Chandra were free to go.

They were free to do whatever they wanted.

"What's our next move?" Chandra asked him in the car he'd borrowed—Parker wouldn't miss it—once they were away from prying eyes.

"Now we eat."

She stared at him.

"Shower?"

More staring.

"Fine, you can sleep first. But then, I get a turn." He grinned.

She sighed. "You're hopeless. How can you act so blasé?"

"Because Parker is gone. Which means the threat to you is gone."

"But what of the woman he called queen?"

The car might have swerved. "What did you say?"

Chandra explained what she'd seen, and he frowned.

"Are you sure she was a dragon?"

"No, I can't be sure. She didn't change into one or anything. The woman I saw had red hair, a red dress, and she had freakishly green eyes."

"That doesn't sound like the current Crimson Sept matriarch."

But Chandra didn't reply. He looked down to see her snoring, her head pillowed against his arm. Safe. For now.

However, the thought that it might not be over for her—and their child—wouldn't stop gnawing at him.

He drove all that night and part of the next day. He drove until he was in familiar territory and ensconced in his grandparents' house, somewhere in British Columbia, guarded by the Mauve Sept. His family.

He'd rejoined them at last. It would provide a layer of protection to his mate and child. As Chandra slept—and the doctors he'd called in tested her blood to see what Parker had wrought—Tomas went looking. Looking for someone to eliminate. He had to get rid of any threat.

When Chandra finally woke, he was waiting, and he had no sooner said, "Good afternoon," than he was shoving a picture in her face. "Is that her?"

She blinked, looking delightfully tousled. "Don't I even get coffee first?"

He sighed. Rising from the side of the bed, he went to the door, stuck his head out, and bellowed, "Breakfast platter. Now."

He returned to sit, and he noted her gaping at him.

"It won't take long."

"Would it have killed you to say please?"

"And disrespect the lessons my grandmother taught me? I don't ask. I command. Especially now that I've returned to the Mauve. Now, you didn't answer. Do you recognize this woman?"

"Who is it?" she asked, a furrow on her brow.

"This is the current Crimson matriarch." Who, while fond of wearing red, opted for sedate outfits, not the form-fitting item Chandra had described.

A shake of her head confirmed her reply. "That's not who I saw."

So who then did Chandra see? Who else colluded with Parker? And with him gone, would they continue, or were the sick games over?

That more than anything was the question they needed to answer. However, Parker was dead, and he'd taken with him so many secrets.

Such as what he'd done to Chandra.

His mate.

The woman carrying his child.

No wonder he'd felt such a connection to her from the moment they met. They were connected. First by science. Then by flesh. And now, their lives would be forever intertwined.

"Forget about Parker and everything else. We have more important things to discuss."

"Such as?"

"You and me." He captured her hand and used it to pull her close. "From the moment we met, I knew there was something different about you."

"So you've said. I'm human, and you're not."

"It's more than that." He ran the tip of his finger along her jaw, stroking the caramel skin. "You are the treasure I've been looking for my entire life."

"You want to own me?"

He groaned. "Why must you question everything I do?"

"Because." She shrugged. "It drove my father a little mad, too."

"I am not your father," Tomas growled.

"Are you sure? You seem to want to control me."

"You think I am the one in control?" He laughed and dropped to his knees. He held out his hands. "Have you not yet realized, doctor, that you are the one with all the power? From the moment we met, my will, my life, my heart, was no longer my own."

Her hand reached out to touch his face. "I don't want to own you either. Can't we both just be together as equals?"

"You mean, have the world revolve around us both? It's an interesting concept."

She laughed. "How about we just love and respect each other?"

He made a face. "Can I respect you later? Because, honestly, right now, I just want to do dirty things to you."

"What kinds of things?" she queried.

"The kind that makes you scream with pleasure." He kissed her lightly. "Things that make you wet." He brushed his mouth over hers again. "Things to show my love."

"Love?" She stopped the kiss and placed her hands on his chest. "Do you love me?"

His turn to freeze. Fear kept him from replying.

She knelt before him and cupped his cheeks. "It's okay. I love you, Tomas."

She loved him. His heart swelled, and he managed to say, and quite arrogantly, too, "I love you more."

Chapter Twenty-four

She couldn't find it in her to chide him. Perhaps he did love her more. He was, after all, a dragon.

And a splendid man. She couldn't help but stare at him as he stripped, denuded them both that they might shower.

She stared at him. Ogled at his perfection. The toned muscles, the smooth, hard flesh.

Her mouth watered as hunger grew within her. A hunger only he could satisfy.

She pressed her hands against his chest, feeling the steady beat of his heart, feeling the scorching heat of his skin.

Slowly, she slid her hands down from his pecs, the palms flat with her fingers spread. His nipples puckered, drawing her attention. She leaned forward, a touch uncertain but wondering what it would feel like to bite one lightly.

The flesh felt strange between her lips, and the soft grind of her teeth on the nub saw Tomas sucking in a sharp breath.

He liked it.

How powerful she felt. She played some more with his nipples, alternating between sucking his tight nubs and rubbing her lips over his shower-slick skin.

As she teased, something poked her in the belly, something hard. Demanding.

Yours.

The word whispered to her, and she smiled as she said, "Mine." She also reached for the shaft looking for attention. It filled her hand, long and thick. She stroked her hand up it, and Tomas hitched a breath. She slid back, and he shuddered.

She had him, literally, in hand. But what if she took him into her mouth? Would he come apart like she did when he licked her?

Dropping to her knees brought her eye level with his erection. One of her hands still gripped it. She watched with curiosity as she stroked it lightly. His cock jerked in response.

Leaning forward, she flicked her tongue out for a lick of the head, swollen and blushing with color. As she licked all around, fingers tangled in her hair. When she pulled him into her mouth, he groaned a long, low rumble. His hips jerked forward, pushing him deeper. She might have choked a little. The man was not small.

But he was fascinating to eat.

The fingers in her hair tightened, a little tug of pain that excited more than it hurt. It encouraged her to take him deeper. Then ease back.

In, suctioning the length of him.

Out, letting her wet lips slide along his slick length.

He filled her so completely, his girth so big that at times her teeth grazed him.

She quite enjoyed giving him pleasure, his sounds of enjoyment, the shudders of his body an aphrodisiac that gave her pleasure, too.

She began to moan around his length, her excitement mounting until he suddenly pulled free of her mouth.

She might have protested, except he was yanking her upright, gently, but firmly. He faced her away from him.

"Put your hands on the wall." A hand in the middle of her back ensured she leaned forward and had to brace herself.

He then tugged her hips back as he pushed apart her feet with his own. Her buttocks were presented to him, and he fit himself behind, the tip of him nudging at her slick sex.

He rubbed it, and her head dropped as her body shivered as it instinctively reacted to the pleasure it knew would come.

At the first deep thrust, she almost came. He'd managed to push himself deep enough to nudge her sweet spot.

He pulled back. Then in. He pushed and gyrated, prolonging her pleasure. His thrusts drove harder and deeper, each stroke more exciting than the last. She panted. She moved, her rhythm matching his, push for push.

All of her gathered itself tight. Relaxed and tensed at the same time. Her orgasm hit, cinching him tightly, keeping him buried in her as wave after wave of pleasure rocked her body.

It rocked him, too, for he came, hot and spurting and murmuring her name.

He carried her to the bed after, curving his body around hers, letting her recover before he insisted they eat.

And then make love again.

And eat some more.

Until his grandmother told them to get outside and enjoy some fresh air before they turned into vampires.

They made love in the woods.

Epilogue

Weeks passed, quiet weeks spent making love with Tomas. Weeks that changed her life as her marriage to Ishaan ended—and not because Tomas ate him.

It took much maneuvering on Chandra's part to convince Tomas to let Ishaan live, but as Chandra reminded Tomas, "Not only does he owe you his life, which is a treasure, but it makes you the bigger dragon."

Tomas liked it when she called him big.

Ishaan didn't waste his second chance. He moved in with his boyfriend and scandalized everyone. Especially Chandra's family, who wailed and complained about the supposed shame Chandra had brought on her family—because surely she was to blame for Ishaan's choice. Dear, Devi, did her father rant about her failures as a daughter. He even showed up in person to cause trouble.

That didn't go over well with Tomas. He wouldn't tell Chandra what he said to her father, but after that, she enjoyed a measure of respect she'd never experienced before.

It helped that Tomas immediately married her, making her a respectable woman instead of one living in sin.

With her family problems more or less solved, she let him meet her *daadee*, along with the rest of her female relatives. They were in awe of her new, very virile husband. It helped he was rich.

Life became quiet, too quiet. Tomas decided to take them for a visit to his aerie. He claimed it was because he wanted to show off his treasures.

More like he wanted to make her scream in pleasure without his grandfather smirking the next day at mealtime.

She didn't mind the change in locale too much because she'd noted Tomas had become very protective of her. He didn't trust the peace. Neither did she. It felt more like the calm before a storm.

The alone time was nice, though. While not a scientist, Tomas was intelligent—and arrogant. But she thought that was cute.

"Come here!" he bellowed.

"I'm not a dog," she retorted. Chandra didn't need to speak loudly. In his aerie, sound carried.

"Take a look and tell me if this is the woman you saw."

"What woman are you talking about?" Chandra asked, leaving the kitchenette part of the cave. It was now fully stocked since they'd chosen to reside here for a while.

Tomas wagged a finger in the direction of the screen, which currently played several channels at once—all of them news channels. "Does that woman look familiar?"

Peeking closer, her eyes widened. "It's her. That's the woman Parker called queen." Chandra perched herself on the arm of the couch. "Who is she? And what is she doing on television?"

"She's not a queen; however, I do think she's about to create history." Tomas slid an arm around her and dumped her into his lap.

The woman on screen tapped the microphone before saying. "Good evening. I am Anastasia, the high priestess for the Keepers of the Golden Faith."

"Who?" someone shouted from a small crowd of reporters.

"Some religious whackjob," snickered another.

For a moment, Anastasia's eyes glowed green. "You will show respect in the presence of your betters. I am the keeper of the dragon faith. And I am here to announce that the day we've foretold is here."

"What day? Did someone forget to give you some meds?"

Her fingers gripped the podium tight. "Remove the human."

"You can't. Freedom of the—" Despite his protests, and that of a few in the crowd, a band of red-haired fellows grabbed the reporter and dragged him out.

The priestess, with flashing green eyes, surveyed the crowd. "Take heed and do not interrupt me. I've called you here as a courtesy so that you might meet someone." Anastasia turned to look into the wings.

The man they'd met as Samael D'Ore emerged, looking the same as he had before, but this time, he appeared on camera. He also seemed to stand taller and wider than before. The man smiled, and in that moment, Tomas must have understood what he'd say because he cursed.

Chandra understood the cursing a moment later as a golden nimbus surrounded Samael.

The priestess announced. "Kneel, humans, for you are in the presence of the last Golden dragon and king. He is the dragon foretold."

Tomas muttered a low, "I'll be damned. They found a living Gold dragon. I think we found Parker's missing puzzle piece."

"What do you mean?"

"You know how the doctors couldn't figure out what Parker did to you?"

"You know?"

Tomas hugged her. "I think I do. It goes back to those glyphs found in that excavation. Parker was recreating a very old spell."

"A spell to do what?"

"Allow wyverns to ascend." His hand splayed over her abdomen, and she heard him in her head.

We were played. Played so hard.

"How? I don't understand." But in a sense, she did. No wonder Parker wanted her back.

"It all makes sense now. How he was preparing you and used me to create the one thing he knew dragons would covet above all else. The one thing that might turn the tide if there is another war."

"You mean…" She looked at her stomach.

"Congratulations, you're about to become the first human mother of a dragon since the Goldens went extinct."

"And you're its daddy." At least he didn't faint when he heard it anymore. Just like he didn't hesitate to love and cherish. The future might loom uncertain before them, but having unleashed the man and the lover, Chandra didn't fear it.

*

Don't show fear. She knew better than to let Anastasia see.

Sue-Ellen waited in a room to the side of the stage, with hands clasped, the picture of demure obedience as Samael was paraded in front of a crowd.

How he must hate it. Sue-Ellen certainly hated all the times Parker had used her for the cameras. She would have avoided this media circus if possible, and yet Anastasia insisted she come. Insisted meant Sue-Ellen didn't really have a choice. She just didn't understand what Anastasia wanted from her now that Parker was out of the picture.

An ignoble death for an ignoble man. She couldn't think of a more fitting end. How her pompous uncle would have hated it.

With Parker gone, Sue-Ellen should leave, and yet she couldn't, not while poor Samael remained a prisoner.

As the larger room outside this one stilled, the silence thick, she dared a peek. Samael—the boy she'd stumbled upon while exploring the lab under her uncle's house—stood before a small crowd in all his Golden glory.

He appeared tall and proud. A golden god for the people. A puppet for an evil priestess.

The man she adored.

The one guy she could never have. Anastasia made it quite clear Samael was destined for greater things than the daughter of a swamp gator.

It didn't stop her from dreaming.

It doesn't have to be a dream. The voice she heard wasn't her own. Funny how optimism sounded just like him.

She sighed, and Samael's head turned as if hearing it. His gaze caught hers. Green fire danced in the depths.

A lip quirked, and she could swear she heard a whispered, *Soon. My precious. My hoard.*

The End of Dragon Unleashed, but be sure to grab the next story: Dragon Foretold

More info at EveLanglais.com

CPSIA information can be obtained
at www.ICGtesting.com
Printed in the USA
LVOW10s2337120617
537815LV00034BA/1829/P